ALSO BY VLADIMIR SOROKIN

The Queue

The Ice Trilogy:
  Bro
  Ice
  23,000

DAY OF THE
OPRICHNIK

DAY OF THE OPRICHNIK

VLADIMIR SOROKIN

TRANSLATED FROM THE RUSSIAN

BY JAMEY GAMBRELL

FARRAR, STRAUS AND GIROUX

NEW YORK

Farrar, Straus and Giroux
18 West 18th Street, New York 10011

Distributed in Canada by D&M Publishers, Inc.
Printed in the United States of America
Originally published in 2006 by Zakharov, Russia, as *Den' oprichnika*
Published in the United States by Farrar, Straus and Giroux
First American edition, 2011

Library of Congress Cataloging-in-Publication Data
Sorokin, Vladimir, 1955–
 [Den' oprichnika. English]
 Day of the oprichnik / Vladimir Sorokin ; translated [from the Russian]
by Jamey Gambrell. — 1st American ed.
    p.   cm.
 Originally published in Russia as Den' oprichnika.
 ISBN 978-0-374-13475-4 (alk. paper)
 I. Gambrell, Jamey.   II. Title.

PG3488.O66D4613 2011
891.73—dc22

                                                    2010039060

Designed by Jonathan D. Lippincott

www.fsgbooks.com

1   3   5   7   9   10   8   6   4   2

DAY OF THE OPRICHNIK

To Grigory Lukyanovich Skuratov-Belsky,
nicknamed Malyuta

Always the same dream: I'm walking across an endless field, a Russian field. Ahead, beyond the receding horizon, I spy a white stallion; I walk toward him, I sense that this stallion is unique, the stallion of all stallions, dazzling, a sorcerer, fleet-footed; I make haste, but cannot overtake him, I quicken my pace, shout, call to him, and realize suddenly: this stallion contains—all life, my entire destiny, my good fortune, that I need him like the very air; and I run, run, run after him, but he recedes with ever measured pace, heeding no one or thing, he is leaving me, leaving forever more, everlastingly, irrevocably, leaving, leaving, leaving . . .

My mobilov awakens me:

One crack of the whip—a scream.

Two—a moan.

Three—the death rattle.

Poyarok recorded it in the Secret Department, when they were torturing the Far Eastern general. It could even wake a corpse.

I put the cold mobilov to my warm, sleepy ear. "Komiaga speaking."

"The best of health, Andrei Danilovich. Korostylev troubling you, sir." The voice of the old clerk from the Ambassadorial Department makes me snap to, and immediately his anxious, mustache-adorned snout appears in the air nearby.

"State your business."

"I beg to remind you: this evening, the reception for the Albanian ambassador is to take place. A dozen or so attendants are required."

"I know," I mutter grumpily, though, truth be told, I'd forgotten.

"Forgive me for troubling you. All in the line of duty."

I put the mobilov on the bedside table. Why the hell is the ambassador's clerk reminding me about attendants? Ah, that's right . . . now the ambassadorials are directing the hand-washing rite . . . I forgot . . . Keeping my eyes closed, I swing my legs over the edge of the bed and shake my head: it feels heavy after yesterday evening. I grope around for the bell, and ring it. Beyond the wall I can hear Fedka jump up from his pallet, bustle about; the dishes clink. I sit still, my head bowed and unwilling to wake up: yesterday, once more I had to fill the cup to the brim, although I solemnly swore to drink and snort only with my own fellows; I did ninety-nine bows of repentance in Uspensky Cathedral and prayed to St. Boniface. Down the drain! What can I do? I cannot refuse the great boyar Kirill Ivanovich. He's intelligent and gives wise, crafty advice. I value a man who's clever, in stark contrast to Poyarok and Sivolai. I could listen to Kirill Ivanovich's sage advice without end, but without his *coke* he isn't very talkative.

Fedka enters:

"Best of health to you, Andrei Danilovich."

I open my eyes.

Fedka is holding a tray. His face is creased and lopsided as it is every morning. He's carrying a traditional hangover assortment: a glass of white kvass, a jigger of vodka, a half-cup of marinated cabbage juice. I drink the juice. It nips my nose and purses my cheekbones. Exhaling, I toss the vodka down in a single gulp. Tears spring to my eyes, blurring Fedka's face. I remember *almost* everything—who I am, where, and what for. I steady my pace, inhaling cautiously. I wash the vodka down with the kvass. The minute of Great Immobility passes. I burp heartily, with an inner groan, and wipe away the tears. Now I remember everything.

Fedka removes the tray and kneels, holding his arm out. Leaning on it, I rise. Fedka smells worse in the morning than in the evening. That's the *truth* of his body, and there's nothing to be done about it. Birch branches and steam baths won't help. Stretching and creaking, I walk over to the iconostasis, light the lampion, and kneel. I say my morning prayers, bow low. Fedka stands behind me; he yawns and crosses himself.

Finishing my prayers, I rise, leaning on Fedka again. I go to the bath. I wash my face in the well water Fedka has prepared with floating slivers of ice. I look at myself in the mirror. My face is slightly puffy, the flare of my nostrils covered with blue veins; my hair is matted. The first touch of gray streaks my temples. A bit early for my age. But such is our job—nothing to be done about it.

Having taken care of my business, large and small, I climb into the Jacuzzi, turn it on, and lean back against the warm, comfortable head support. I look at the mural on the ceiling: girls picking cherries in a garden. It's soothing. I look at the girlish legs, at the baskets of ripe cherries. Water fills the bath, foaming and gurgling around my body. The vodka inside and the foam outside gradually bring me to my senses. After a quarter hour, the gurgling stops. I lie there a bit longer. I press a button. Fedka enters with a towel and robe. He helps me climb out of the

Jacuzzi, covers me with the towel, and wraps me in the robe. I move on into the dining room. Tanyusha is already serving breakfast. The news bubble is on the far wall. I give the command:

"News!"

The bubble flashes and the sky blue, white, and red flag of the Motherland with the gold two-headed eagle unfurls; the bells of the church of Ivan the Great ring. Sipping tea with raspberries, I watch the news: departmental clerks and district councils in the North Caucasus section of the Southern Wall have been stealing again. The Far Eastern Pipeline will remain closed until petition from the Japanese. The Chinese are enlarging their settlements in Krasnoyarsk and Novosibirsk. The trial of the moneychangers from the Urals' Treasury continues. The Tatars are building a smart palace in honor of His Majesty's anniversary. Those featherbrains from the Healer's Academy are completing work on the aging gene. The Muromsk psaltery players will give two concerts in our Whitestone Kremlin. Count Trifon Bagrationovich Golitsyn beat his young wife. In January there will be no flogging on Sennaya Square in St. Petrograd. The ruble's up another half-kopeck against the yuan.

Tanyusha serves cheese pancakes, steamed turnips in honey, and cranberry *kissel*. Unlike Fedka, Tanyusha is fair of face and fragrant. Her skirts rustle pleasantly.

The strong tea and cranberry return me to life. I break into a healthy sweat. Tanyusha hands me a towel that she embroidered. I wipe my face, stand, cross myself, and thank the Lord for the meal.

It's time to get down to business.

The barber, a newcomer, is already waiting in the dressing room, to which I proceed. Silent, stocky Samson bows and seats me in front of the mirror; he massages my face and rubs my neck with lavender oil. His hands, like those of all barbers, are unpleasant. But I disagree in principle with the cynic Mandelstam—the authorities are in no way "repellent, like the hands of a beard-cutter." They're lovely and appealing, like the womb of a virgin needleworker embroidering gold-threaded fancywork. And the hands of a beard-cutter are . . . well, what can you do—women are not allowed to shave our beards. From an orange spray can labeled "Genghis Khan," Samson spreads foam on my cheeks with extreme precision; without touching my beautiful, narrow beard he picks up the razor and sharpens it on the strop in sweeping strokes. He takes aim, tucks in his lower lip, and begins to remove the foam from my face, evenly and smoothly. I look at myself. My cheeks *aren't very fresh* anymore. These last two years I've lost half a pood. Circles under my eyes are now the norm. All of us suffer from chronic lack of sleep. Last night was no exception.

Exchanging his razor blade for an electric machine, Samson deftly trims my poleaxe-shaped beard.

I wink at myself sternly: "A good morning to you, Komiaga!"

The unpleasant hands place a hot cloth, steeped in mint, on my face. Samson wipes it meticulously, rouges my cheeks, curls and glazes my forelock, shakes a generous helping of gold powder on it, and adorns my right ear with a heavy gold earring in the shape of a clapperless bell. We are the only ones to wear these earrings. No Zemstvo representative, department scribe, Duma member, or aristocratic bastard would dare wear this bell even at a Christmas masquerade.

Samson sprays my head with Wild Apple, bows silently, and leaves—his barber's work is done. Then Fedka appears. His mug is still furrowed, but he's had time to change his shirt, brush his teeth, and wash his hands. He's ready for my robing. I place my palm on the lock of my wardrobe. The lock beeps, its red light blinks, and the oak door slides to the side. Each morning I see my eighteen caftans. The very sight of them is invigorating. Today is a regular workday. Therefore, working clothes.

"Business," I tell Fedka.

He takes a robe out of the wardrobe and begins to dress me: first, a white undergarment embroidered with crosses, a red shirt with collar buttons on the side, a brocade jacket with weasel trim, embroidered with gold and silver thread, velvet pants, red boots of Moroccan leather fashioned with wrought copper soles. Over my brocade jacket, Fedka places a black, floor-length, wadded cotton caftan made of rough broadcloth.

Glancing at myself in the mirror, I close the wardrobe.

In the hall the clock reads: 08:03. There's time. Already awaited by my domestic entourage: Nanny with an icon of St. George the Dragonslayer, Fedka with my hat and girdle. I put on the black velvet hat with sable trim, and allow myself to be girdled with a wide leather belt. On the left side of the strap is a dagger in a scabbard, on the right a Rebroff in a wooden holster. Nanny makes the sign of the cross over me, muttering at the same time:

"Andryushenka, may our Most Holy Mother of God, Saint Nikola, and all the Optina Elders protect you!"

Her pointed chin trembles, her blue eyes tear with tenderness. I cross myself and kiss the icon of St. George. Nanny tucks the prayer "He that dwelleth in the secret place of the most High" in my pocket—it was embroidered by the nuns of Novodevichy Monastery in gold on a black ribbon. I never leave for work without this prayer.

"Grant victory over our foes . . ." Fedka mumbles as he crosses himself.

Anastasia peeks out of the back maid's room: a red and white *sarafan*, blond braid falling over the right shoulder, and emerald eyes. But the glow of her crimson cheeks betrays her: she's worried. She lowers her eyes, bows ardently, her high breasts trembling, and hides behind the oak doorpost. Instantly I feel my heart *surge* at the sight of the girlish bow: the night before last, the night was flung open by a sultry darkness, was revived by a sweet moan in the ears, a warm girlish body pressed closed, she whispered passionately, like blood flew through the veins.

But—work comes first.

And today we're up to our ears in work. And then there's this Albanian ambassador . . .

I go into the outer vestibule. The servants have all lined up—the farmyard workers, the cook, the chef, the yardman, the game warden, the guards, the housekeeper:

"The best of health to you, Andrei Danilovich!"

They bow to the waist. I nod at them as I pass. The floorboards creak. They open the forged iron door. I go out into the courtyard. The day has turned out sunny, nippy with frost. Some snow fell overnight—on the fir trees, on the fence, on the guard tower. Ah, how I love the snow! It covers the earth's shame. And the soul is purer for it.

Squinting in the sun, I look around the courtyard: the granary, the hay barn, the stables—everything's orderly, solid, and well built. A shaggy dog strains at its chain, the borzois yelp in the kennel behind the house, the rooster crows in the shed. The courtyard has been swept clean, the snowdrifts are as neat as tall Easter cakes. My Mercedov stands at the gates—crimson like my shirt, stocky, and clean. Its clear glass shines. And right next to it the groom Timokha stands with a dog's head in hand; he waits, and bows:

"Andrei Danilovich, your approval!"

He shows me the dog's head of the day: a shaggy wolfhound, eyes rolled back, tongue touched with hoarfrost, strong yellow teeth. It will do.

"Carry on!"

Timokha fastens the head of the dog deftly to the hood of

the Mercedov, the oprichnina broom to the trunk of the car. I place my palm on the Mercedov's lock; the transparent roof floats upward. I settle into the reclining black leather seat. I buckle the belt. Turn on the motor. The plank gates open in front of me. Out I drive, flying along the narrow straight road flanked by an old, snow-covered spruce forest. In the rearview mirror I see my homestead receding. A good house, with a heart and soul. I've been living in it for only seven months, yet it feels as though I was born and grew up there. The property used to belong to a comrade moneychanger at the Treasury: Gorokhov, Stepan Ignatievich. When he fell into disgrace during the Great Treasury Purge and exposed himself, we took him in hand. During that hot summer a good number of Treasury heads rolled. Bobrov and five of his henchmen were paraded through Moscow in an iron cage, then flogged with the rod and beheaded on Lobnoe Mesto in Red Square. Half of the Treasury was exiled from Moscow beyond the Urals. There was a lot of work . . . It was back then that Gorokhov, as was befitting, was dragged with his mug in the dung; banknotes were stuffed in his mouth, it was sewn shut, a candle was shoved up his ass, and he was hung on the gates of the estate. We were told not to touch the family. Then the property was transferred to me. His Majesty is just. And thank God.

The road bears right.

I drive out onto the Rublyov highway. It's a good road, two stories, ten lanes. I maneuver into the left one, the red lane. This is our lane. The government's. As long as I live and serve the state, I will drive in it.

Cars yield, envying the oprichnik's red Mercedov with its dog's head. I cut through the air of the Moscow region with a whistle, flooring the pedal. The duty policeman looks respectfully to the side.

I give a command:

"Radio Rus."

The soft voice of a young woman speaks up:

"The best of health to you, Andrei Danilovich. What is your listening pleasure?"

I already know the news. When you've got a hangover the soul desires a good song:

"Sing me the one about the steppe and the eagle."

"It will be done."

The psaltery players start off smoothly, little bells tinkle, a larger silver bell chimes:

"Oy, the steppe is broad and wide,
Our Russian steppe is free, hey!
Wide and broad, our mother fair
She reaches out to me, hey!
O Russian steppe, you're wide,
Your span is far and free, hey!
O Mother fair, your lovely hand
Reaches far across the land.
O Russian eagle, it's not you I see,
Rising o'er the steppe so free,
'Tis but a Cossack of the Don
Out to have his fun, hey!"

The Kremlin Red Banner Choir is singing. The choir sings powerfully, beautifully. The song resounds, and I can feel tears welling up. The Mercedov races toward our Whitestone Kremlin; villages and estates flash by. The sun shines on snow-covered spruce trees. The soul revives, is purified, and desires the lofty . . .

"O Eagle, do not fly so low!
So low unto the ground,
O Cossack, do not wander close,
So close unto the shore's sweet sound!"

I'd like to drive into Moscow listening to that song, but I'm interrupted. Posokha calls. His sleek kisser appears in a rainbow frame.

"Oh, go to . . ." I mutter, turning off the song.
"Komiaga!"
"What do you want?"
"Work and Word, We Live to Serve!"
"Well?"

"There's been a bit of a hitch with the nobleman."

"How's that?"

"They weren't able to plant the goods on him last night."

"What's going on with all of you?! Why didn't you say anything, you chicken ass?"

"We waited till the very end, but his security is top-notch, three caps."

"Batya knows?"

"Nunh-unh. Komiaga, please tell Batya, will you? He's still mad at me because of the tradesmen. I'm scared. I'll make it up to you, don't worry."

I call Batya. His wide, red-bearded face appears to the right of the steering wheel.

"Hello, Batya."

"Greetings, Komiaga. Ready?"

"I'm always ready, Batya, but our guys put their foot in it. They couldn't plant any treasonous literature on the nobleman."

"Oh, we don't need to anymore." Batya yawns, showing his strong, healthy teeth. "He can be toppled without that. He's *naked*. Only here's the thing: don't mutilate the family, got it?"

"Got it." I nod, turning off Batya and turning on Posokha. "You hear that?"

"I heard!" He grins with relief. "Thank the Lord . . ."

"The Lord has nothing to do with it. Thank His Majesty."

"Work and Word!"

"And don't be late, you bum."

"I'm already here."

I turn onto First Uspensky highway. Here the trees are even higher than ours: ancient, centuries-old firs. They have seen much in their time. They remember: they remember the Red Troubles, they remember the White Troubles, they remember the Gray Troubles, they remember the Rebirth of Rus. They remember the Transformation as well. We'll be ash and fly off to other worlds, but the glorious firs of the Moscow region will stand straight, their dignified branches swaying . . .

Hmmm . . . so that's how things shook out with the nobleman! No need to charge him with mutiny now. The same thing happened with Prozorovsky last week; now with this one . . . His Majesty is tough with the nobility. All right and proper. When you've lost your head, you don't fret about your hair. In for a penny, in for a pound. If you raise the axe, let it fall!

I see two of our fellows ahead in red Mercedovs. I catch up and slow down. We drive in procession. We turn. We drive a bit farther and arrive at the gates of hereditary nobleman Ivan Ivanovich Kunitsyn's estate. Eight of our cars are already there. Posokha is here, Khrul, Sivolai, Pogoda, Okhlop, Ziabel, Nagul, and Kreplo. Batya sent the heavies for this affair. That's right, Batya. Kunitsyn's a hard nut. To crack him you need the knack.

I park, get out of the car, open the trunk, and retrieve my wooden cudgel. The others are standing around, waiting for the command. Batya's not here, so I'm in charge. We greet one another professionally. I look at the fence: the Streltsy from the Secret Department, sent as backup, are stationed all along the perimeter, in the forest. The estate has been surrounded since last night by His Majesty's order. Not even a malicious mouse could scurry in, nor a wily mosquito escape.

But the nobleman's gates are strong. Poyarok, who arrived when I did, rings the bell:

"Ivan Ivanych, open up. Open up while you're still in one piece!"

"Without Duma officials you'll not enter, murderers!" comes a voice out of the speaker.

"It'll only be worse, Ivan Ivanych!"

"It won't get any worse for me, you curs!"

What's true is true. It can only get worse in the Secret Department. But Ivan Ivanovich doesn't need to go there anymore. We'll deal with him on our own. Our people are waiting. It's time!

I walk up to the gates. The oprichniks stand still. I pound on the gates with my cudgel the first time:

"Woe to this home!"

I pound the second time:

"Woe to this home!"

I pound the third time:

"Woe to this home!"

And the oprichnina stirs:

"Work and Word! We Live to Serve!"

"Hail! Work and Word!!"

"Work and Word!!"

"Hail! Hail! Hail!"

I slap Poyarok on the shoulder:

"Go to it!"

Poyarok and Sivolai bustle about, setting a firecracker between the gates. Everyone moves back and plugs his ears.

There's an explosion and the oak gates turn to kindling. We break in with our cudgels. Now we face the nobleman's guards with their staves. Firearms are not allowed for defense; otherwise the Streltsy would cut the lot of them down with their cold-firing ray guns. And according to the law of the Duma, whatever servant raises a staff in defense against a *raid*, he shall not fall into disgrace.

We rush in. Ivan Ivanovich has a wealthy estate, the courtyard is spacious. There's room to move around. A bunch of guards and servants awaits us. They have three dogs on chains, raring to get at us. Fighting with a horde like this is grave business. We'll have to negotiate. A sly approach is needed to run state affairs. I raise my hand:

"Listen here! Your master won't leave here alive anyway!"

"We know!" the guards shout. "We'll still have to defend ourselves against you!"

"Just wait a minute! Let's each choose one of our own for single combat! If you win, you leave without injury, with your belongings! If we win—we get everything you have!"

The guards begin to think. And Sivolai says:

"Come on, say yes while we're still friendly. We'll kick you out when our backup arrives! No one can hold out against the oprichnina!"

They talk among themselves, then shout:

"All right. What're our weapons?"

"Fists!" I answer.

Their combatant comes forward: an enormous stable hand with a mug like a pumpkin. He throws off his sheepskin coat, pulls on his leather sleeves, and wipes the snot dripping from his nose. But we're prepared—Pogoda throws his black caftan to Sivolai, shakes his weasel-trimmed hat, tosses off his brocade jacket, rolls his valiant shoulders covered in crimson silk, winks at me, and steps forward. Even our Maslo is a kid when it comes to fist-fighting. Pogoda is short, but wide in the shoulders, strong-boned, firm of grip, shifty. Hard to land one on his smooth kisser. For him it's easy as pie to pulverize someone to chopped meat.

Pogoda looks at his opponent with mischief in his eyes, squinting, playing with his silken belt.

"So then, you clumsy oaf, ready for a trouncing?"

"Don't brag when you go into battle, oprichnik!"

Pogoda and the stable hand circle, sizing each other up. They're dressed differently, come from different stations, serve different masters, but if you look close—they're made of the same Russian dough. Tough Russian people.

We're in a circle, right up close to the servants. This is the usual in a fist-fighting arena. Here everyone's equal—the serf and the nobleman, the oprichnik and the scribe. The fist is its own lord and master.

Pogoda chuckles and winks at the stable hand. He loosens his valiant shoulders, rolling them up and down. The lout can't take it; he rushes him with a swing of his hefty fist. Pogoda crouches and the stable hand takes a short jab in the gut. The guy gasps, but steadies himself. Pogoda dances around, mincing like a tart. He rocks back and forth, sticks out his pink tongue. The stable hand doesn't care for dancing, he grunts and swings again. But Pogoda's ready for him—left punch to the jaw, right punch to the ribs. Crack! Crack! The ribs fracture. And Pogoda again dodges the meaty fist. The stable hand roars like a bear and waves his enormous arms, losing his gloves. And all for naught: once more he takes it in the gut and on the nose. Crack! The husky fellow steps back, staggering like a bear that doesn't hibernate. He locks his hands together, roars, and cleaves the frosty air. Again all for naught! Bam! Bam! Bam! Pogoda's fists are swift: the stable hand's mug is already bloody, he's got a black eye, and his nose is running red. Crimson drops fly, sparkling like rubies in the winter sun as they fall on the trampled snow.

The servants look grim. Our guys wink back and forth. The stable hand sways, his broken nose drips, and he spits out a bunch of teeth. Another blow, and another. The husky fellow stumbles backward, waves Pogoda away like a bear cub shooing bees. But Pogoda doesn't stop: again! again! The oprichnik hits hard and strong. We whistle and hoot. The last punch, another tooth breaker. The stable hand falls flat on his back. Pogoda steps on his chest with his fashionable boot, draws a knife out of its sheath, and snick! Right across his face with a flourish! For the art of it. That's the way it always goes *nowadays*. It's like slicing through butter.

The servants are quiet. The lout grabs his slit mug; blood runs through his fingers.

Pogoda puts his knife away and spits on the fallen servant. He winks at all the others:

"Pah! His mug is bloody!"

These are *famous* words. We always say them. That's the *custom*.

Now it's time to dot the i's. I lift my cudgel.

"On your knees, you lumbering louts!"

At moments like these, everything is transparent. Oy, how you can see through Russian people. Faces, faces of the servants, struck dumb. Simple Russian faces. How I love to watch them at such moments, the *moment of truth*. Right now, they're a mirror. In which we are reflected. And the winter sunlight.

Thank God this mirror hasn't grown dim, hasn't darkened with time.

The servants fall on their knees.

Our guys relax and start moving around. Batya calls right away: he's following everything from his residence in Moscow.

"Well done!"

"We serve Russia, Batya! What about the house?"

"For demolition."

Demolition? Now, that's new . . . Usually a *suppressed* mansion or estate is kept. And the former servants stay on under the new master. Like my home. We look at each other. Batya grins a white-toothed grin.

"Why so quiet? It's an order: clear the place."

"We'll do it, Batya!"

Aha . . . Clear the place. That means the *red rooster*. This hasn't happened in a blue moon. But—an order is an order. Not open for discussion. I order the servants:

"Each of you can take a sack of goods! We're giving you two minutes!"

They already know that the house is lost. They jump up, run off, disappear into all the nooks and crannies to grab whatever they've saved and whatever they happen upon. Meanwhile our guys are looking the house over: gratings, iron doors, walls of red brick. Everything good and solid. Good brickwork, smooth. The curtains on the windows are drawn, but not tightly: eyes dart through the cracks. That's where the homefire is, behind the bars, a farewell warmth, hiding, trembling with deadly trepidation. Oh, how sweet it would be to penetrate that cozy place, how sweet to pluck that farewell fear out!

The servants gather a sack of goods each. They file out obediently, like pilgrims. We let them through the gates. And there, at the gap, the Streltsy are on duty with their ray guns. The servants leave the mansion compound, looking back. Look back, you uncouth louts, we don't mind. It's our time now. We surround the house, banging our cudgels on the bars, on the walls:

"Hail!"

"Hail!"

"Hail!"

Then we circle it three times, following the sun's orbit.

"Woe to this house!"

"Woe to this house!"

"Woe to this house!"

Poyarok affixes a firecracker to the iron door. We stand back and cover our ears with our gloves. Blast!—and there's no door. But after the first door there's another door—made of wood. Sivolai gets out a ray saw. There's a whining, and a blue flame furiously punctures the door like a thin knitting needle—and the section of door falls through.

We enter leisurely. There's no reason to hurry now.

Inside, it's quiet, peaceful. The nobleman has a good house, very comfortable. The parlor is decorated in the Chinese style—sofas, rugs, small low tables, human-size vases, scrolls, dragons on silk and carved in jade. The news bubbles are also Chinese, bordered with black bent wood. The room smells of Eastern aromas. It is the fashion, what can you do about it . . . We climb a wide staircase fitted in Chinese carpet. Now we get to the familiar smells—icon oil lamps entice, good old-fashioned wood, old books, valerian root. A quality mansion, made of logs, well caulked. With towels, icon cases, trunks, chests of drawers, samovars, and tile stoves. We wander through the rooms. No one around. Could that worm really have gotten away? We run our cudgels under the beds, pull off bedclothes, smash the wardrobes. The master is nowhere to be found.

"Didn't fly up the chimney, did he?" Posokha mutters.

"Gotta be a secret entrance in the house somewhere," grumbles Kreplo, rummaging through the chests of drawers with his cudgel.

"The fence is surrounded by Streltsy, where can he go?" I object.

We climb up to the attic. There's a winter garden, bathhouse stones, a wall of water, exercise machines, an observatory. Nowadays they all have observatories . . . That's something I don't get: astronomy and astrology are great sciences, it's true, but what does a telescope have to do with it? It's not a fortune-telling book! The demand for telescopes within the Kremlin's White City is simply mind-boggling, I can't wrap my head around it. Even Batya set up a telescope in his mansion. True, he doesn't have time to look through it.

Posokha might as well be reading my thoughts:

"These nobles and moneychangers—indulging in star-goggling. Whadda they lookin' for? Their own death?"

"Maybe God?" Khrul chuckles, knocking his cudgel against a palm tree.

"Don't blaspheme!" Batya's voice calls him to order.

"Forgive me, Batya." Khrul crosses himself. "It was the devil's work."

"Why are you all searching around the old-fashioned way, boys?" Batya isn't appeased. "Turn on the 'searcher'!"

We turn on the "searcher." It beeps and points to the first floor. We go down. The "searcher" leads us to two Chinese vases. Large vases, standing on the floor, taller than me. We look at one another and wink. I nod at Khrul and Sivolai. They swing back and—crash! The cudgels hit the vases! The porcelain is exceptionally fine, like the eggshell of some enormous dragon, and it flies in all directions. And from these eggs, like Castor and Pollux—the noble's children tumble out! They roll around the carpet like peas and start howling. Three, four, six. All of them blond, about a year apart, one smaller than the next.

"Well, look what we've got here!" The invisible Batya laughs. "Ay ay ay, look what that crook concocted!"

"He was so scared he went completely batty!" Sivolai said, leering at the children.

His grin is *nasty*. But that's the way it is. We don't touch the little ones . . . No, not unless there's an order to *squash the innards*, that's something different. Otherwise—we don't need any extra blood-spilling.

Our fellows catch the shrieking children like willow grouse, and carry them out under their arms. Outside, the lame tax collector, Averian Trofimich, has arrived from the orphanage in his yellow bus. He'll place the little ones, he won't let them fall between the cracks; he'll raise them to be honest citizens of a great country.

To catch the nobles' wives we use the cries of the children as bait; Kunitsyn's spouse couldn't stand it, she howled from her hiding place. Women's hearts aren't made of stone. We follow the cry—it leads to the kitchen. We enter at a leisurely pace. We look around. Ivan Ivanovich has a good kitchen. Spacious and intelligently laid out. You've got your preparation table, and stove-tops, and steel shelves, and glass ones with dishes and spices, and complicated ovens with hot and cold rays and all kinds of foreign high-tech, and tricky ventilation systems, and transparent refrigerators lit from below. There's any type of knife you could want, and in the middle—a wide, white Russian tile oven. Good for Ivan Ivanovich. What kind of Russian Orthodox repast can you have without cabbage soup and buckwheat porridge? Can a foreign oven really bake savory pies like a Russian oven? Would milk curdle the right way? And what about bread, the father and mother? Russian bread needs to be baked in a Russian oven—the poorest beggar will tell you that.

The mouth of the copper oven door is ajar; Poyarok knocks on it with a bent finger:

"The gray wolf has come, he's brought some pies for you. Knock-knock, who's hiding in the oven?"

From behind the door come a woman's wail and a man's cussing. Ivan Ivanovich is cross at his wife for giving them away with her cry. Well, of course, what do you expect? Women's hearts are sensitive, that's why we love them.

Poyarok removes the damper door, takes out stove tongs and a poker, and drags the noble and his spouse out into God's light. The noble's hands are immediately tied, and a gag stuffed in his mouth. He's pushed by his elbows out into the yard. And the wife . . . we'll handle the wife in a merrier fashion. *That's the way it's usually done.* She's tied to the butcher table. Ivan Ivanovich's wife is a beauty: pleasing in form, fair of face, bosomy, well buttocked, spunky. But first—the nobleman. We all rush out of the house into the yard. Ziabel and Kreplo are already standing, waiting with their birch brooms, and Nagul with his soaped rope. The oprichniks drag the noble by the legs from the porch to the gates on his last outing. Ziabel and Kreplo sweep the tracks after him so that no trace of His Majesty's enemy remains in Russia. Nagul has already climbed the gates and nimbly set up the rope; not the first time he's hung Russia's foes. We also stand under the gates, and lift the noble.

"Work and Word!!"

In the blink of an eye Ivan Ivanovich is swaying in the noose, wheezing, sniffling, jerking, farting his farewell. We remove our hats and cross ourselves. We put them back on. We wait until the noble has given up the ghost.

One third of our work is done. Now—the wife. We return to the house.

"Don't kill her!"—Batya's voice warns us, *as always*.

"Got it, Batya!"

This work is—passionate, and absolutely necessary. It gives us more strength to overcome the enemies of the Russian state. Even this *succulent* work requires a certain seriousness. You have to start and *finish* by seniority. So this time, I'm first. The widow of the now deceased Ivan Ivanovich thrashes on the table, screaming and moaning. I rip off her dress, tear off her intricate lace undergarments. Poyarok and Sivolai force her smooth, white, well-tended legs open, and hold them. I love women's legs, especially their thighs and toes. The wife of Ivan Ivanovich has pale thighs, a bit cold, but her toes are tender, well formed, with well-kept toenails covered in pink nail polish. Her weak legs squirm in the strong oprichnik hands, and a slight shiver runs through her toes; they splay and stiffen from tension and fear. Poyarok and Sivolai know my weaknesses: they hold her tender, trembling foot near my mouth; I gather the shaking toes between my lips, and launch my bald ferret right into her womb.

How sweet!

The widow jerks and squeals like a live pink piglet on a

red-hot spit. I dig my teeth into her foot. She screams and thrashes on the table. But I bring my *succulent* work to completion meticulously and implacably.

"Hail! Hail!" the oprichniks mutter, turning away.

Important work.

Necessary work.

Good work.

Without this work, a *raid* is like a stallion without a rider . . . without reins . . . a white stallion, white knight, white stallion . . . beautiful . . . brilliant . . . bewitched stallion . . . a tender stallion-galleon . . . a sugar-sweet stallion with no rider . . . no reins . . . no reins . . . with a white fiend . . . a sweet fiend . . . a fiend of sugar reigns . . . no rider . . . no rain, no galleon-stallion, galloping and no reins, no sugar reins, no sugary rains . . . galleon galloping where the white sugar fiend reigns and the distant sugar rains, faraway, the reins galloping, trotting, sugar reins, galloping, cantering, sugary, cantering to the sugary, to the canterer, how faaar to the sugary caaaantering cuuuuuunnnnnnnttt!

How sweet to leave one's own seed in the womb of the wife of an enemy of the state.

Sweeter than cutting off the heads of the enemies themselves.

The widow's tender toes fall out of my mouth.

Colorful rainbows swim before my eyes.

I turn over my place to Posokha. His member has freshwater pearls sewn in it; the pattern resembles Ilya Muromets's diamond-shaped vestments.

Oh my, the noble's got the heat up high. I go out onto the porch and sit down on the bench. The children have already been taken away. Spurts of blood on the snow are all that remain of the slashed and beaten stable hand. The Streltsy dawdle about the gate, looking at the noble swinging in the breeze. I take out a pack of Motherland and light up. I'm fighting this heathen habit. Although I've reduced the number of cigarettes to seven a day, I just don't have the willpower to quit permanently. Father Paisii prayed for me, commanded me to read the canon of repentance. It didn't help . . . The smoke lies across a frosty breeze. The sun is still shining, the snow and sun winking at each other. I love winter. The cold clears the head, invigorates the blood. In the Russian winter state affairs get done faster, go more smoothly.

Posokha comes out onto the porch: his huge lips are swollen, saliva is about to drip from them, his eyes are dazed, and there's no way he can zip his pants up over his purplish hardworked member. He stands with his legs spread out and does his business. A book falls out from under his caftan. I pick it up. I open it—Afanasev's *Secret Tale*. I read the epigraph:

In those far-off olden times,
When Sacred Russia had no knives,
Carving meat was done with pricks.

This little book has been read till there are holes in it; it's tattered and grease almost oozes from its pages.

"What are you reading, you impudent lout?" I slap Posokha on the forehead with the book. "If Batya sees it—he'll throw you out of the oprichnina!"

"I'm sorry, Komiaga, the devil made me do it," Posokha mutters.

"You're walking along a knife edge, you dimwit! This obscene stuff is subversive. There were purges in the Printing Department on account of these sorts of books. Is that where you picked it up?"

"I wasn't in the oprichnina then. I came across it in the house of one of them generals. The devil nudged me."

"Just understand, you idiot, we're guards. We have to keep our minds cold and our hearts pure."

"I understand, I understand . . ." Posokha scratched the black hair under his hat, in boredom.

"His Majesty can't stand cusswords."

"I know."

"Well, if you know—burn that indecent book!"

"I'll burn it, Komiaga, here, I'll swear on it"—and he crosses himself in a sweeping gesture, hiding the book.

Nagul and Okhlop come out. As the door closes behind them I hear the moans of the noble's widow.

"What a fine bitch!" Okhlop spits, and cocks his cap back.

"They won't bang her to death, will they?" I ask, stubbing out my butt on the bench.

"I don't think so . . ." The wide-faced smiling Nagul blows his nose into a white handkerchief lovingly embroidered by someone.

Ziabel soon appears. After a roll in the hay he's always excited and garrulous. Like me, Ziabel attended university, has a higher education.

"How glorious it is to destroy Russia's enemies, don't you know," he mutters, taking out a pack of unfiltered Rodina. "Genghis Khan used to say that the greatest pleasure on earth was to conquer your enemies, plunder their possessions, ride their horses, and love their wives. What a wise man he was!"

The fingers of Nagul, Okhlop, and Ziabel reach into the pack of Rodina. I take out my flint-fire with cold blue flame and let them light up.

"It looks like you're all hooked on this devilish *weed*. Do you know that tobacco is damned forever by the seven saintly stones?"

"We know, Komiaga." Nagul grins, taking a toke on his cigarette.

"You're smoking Satan's incense, oprichniks. The devil taught people to smoke tobacco so they would praise him with incense. Every cigarette is incense to the glory of the foul fiend."

"But one defrocked monk told me, 'He who does tobacco smoke / is sure to be Christ's bloke,'" Okhlop objects.

"And the Cossack lieutenant in our regiment always said, 'Smoked meat keeps longer.'" Posokha sighs as he takes a cigarette.

"You numbskulls, you blockheads! Our Majesty doesn't smoke," I tell them. "Batya quit, too. We have to watch the cleanliness of our lungs, too. And our tongues."

They smoke silently, listening.

The door opens and the rest of the lot stagger out with the noble's wife. She's naked, unconscious, wrapped in a sheepskin coat. For us, tumbling a woman is a special kind of work.

"Is she alive?"

"They rarely die from it!" Pogoda smiles. "It's not the rack, after all."

I take her senseless hand. There's a pulse.

"All right, then. Drop the woman off at her family's."

"You got it."

They take her out. It's time to finish up. The oprichniks keep glancing at the house: it's wealthy, full of goods. But since the mansion is to be demolished by order of His Majesty, no stealing is allowed. It's the law. All the goods go to His Majesty's *red rooster.*

I nod to Ziabel; he's our guy for fire.

"Take over!"

He takes his Rebroff out of the holster and puts a bottle-shaped attachment on the barrel. We move away from the house. Ziabel aims at the window and shoots. The windowpane splinters and shatters. We move farther away from the house. We stand in a half-circle, take our daggers out of their scabbards, raise them up, lower them, and aim them at the house.

"Woe to this house!"

"Woe to this house!"

"Woe to this house!"

There's an explosion. The flames are thick, belching out the windows. Shards of glass, frames, and grates fall on the snow. The mansion has been taken. His Majesty's *red rooster* has come to call.

"Well done!" Batya's face appears in the frosty air, in a rainbow frame. "Let the Streltsy go, and get yourselves to prayer in Uspensky!"

All's well that ends well. When work is done—we pray in the sun.

We exit, avoiding the hanging corpse. On the other side of the gates the Streltsy are pushing back reporters. They stand there with their cameras, champing at the bit to take pictures of the fire. Now they're allowed in. Since the News Decree, after that memorable November, it's all right. I wave to the lieutenant. The cameras focus on the fire, on the hanging nobleman. In every house, in every news bubble, Russian Orthodox people will know and see the power of His Majesty and the state.

As His Majesty says:

"Law and order—resurrected from the Gray Ashes, that's what Holy Rus stands on and will always stand on."

It's the sacred truth!

In Uspensky Cathedral, as always, the atmosphere is murky, muggy, and majestic. Candles burn, the icons' gold casings shine, the censer smokes in the hand of narrow-shouldered Father Juvenale, his delicate voice echoes; the bass voice of the fat, black-bearded deacon booms from the choir steps. We stand in crowded rows—all the oprichniks of Moscow. Batya is here, and Yerokha, his right hand, and Mosol, his left hand. And we're all native Muscovites, including me. We're the backbone. We also have the young ones. His Majesty is the only one absent. On Mondays he usually graces us with his presence—he comes to pray with us. But today our sun isn't here. His Majesty, our head of state, is completely immersed in state affairs. Or he might be in the Church of the Deposition of the Robe of the Virgin Mary, his domestic temple, praying for Sacred Russia. His Majesty's will is law and mystery. And thank God.

It's a normal day today, Monday. The usual service. The Epiphany has passed, sleighs have been ridden along the Moscow River, the cross has been lowered in an ice hole. Under a silver gazebo, twined 'round with spruce boughs, infants have been baptized, we ourselves have taken a dip in the icy water, fired the cannons, bowed to His Majesty and Her Highness, feasted in the Granite Chamber with the Kremlin entourage and the Inner Circle. Now there are no holidays until Candlemas, just plain workdays. There are jobs to do.

"And God will be resurrected and His enemies shall be in ruins . . ." reads Father Juvenale.

We cross ourselves and bow. I pray to my favorite icon, the Savior of the Ardent Eye; I tremble before the fury of our Savior's eyes. Formidable is our Savior, immovable in His Judgment. I gather strength for battle from His stern gaze, I fortify my spirit, train my nature. I amass hatred for our enemies. I sharpen my mind and reason.

Yes, all God's and His Majesty's enemies shall be scattered.

"Grant victory over all who oppose us . . ."

There are plenty of opponents, that's true. As soon as Russia rose from the Gray Ashes, as soon as she became aware of herself, as soon as His Majesty, Father Nikolai Platonovich, laid the foundation stone of the Western Wall sixteen years ago, as soon as we began to fence ourselves off from the foreign without and the demon within—opponents began to crawl out of the cracks like noxious centipedes. A truly great idea breeds great resistance. Our state has always had enemies inside and out, but the battle was never so intense as during the period of Holy Russia's Revival. More than one head rolled on the block at Lobnoe Mesto during those sixteen years, more than one train carried our foes and their families beyond the Urals, more than one *red rooster* crowed at dawn in a noble's mansion, more than one general farted on the rack in the Secret Department, more than one denunciation was dropped in the Work and Word! box at Lubianka, more than one moneychanger had his mouth stuffed with the bills of his ill-gotten gains, more than one clerk was dunked in boiling water, more than one foreign envoy was escorted out of Moscow by three shameful yellow Mercedovs, more than one reporter was pushed from the tower at Ostankino with goose feathers up his ass, more than one hackneyed rabble-rouser of a writer was drowned in the Moscow River, more than one nobleman's widow was dropped off at her parents' home, naked and unconscious, wrapped in a sheepskin . . .

Each time I stand in Uspensky Cathedral with a candle in my hand, I think secret, treasonous thoughts on one subject: What if we didn't exist? Would His Majesty be able to manage on his own? Would the Streltsy, the Secret Department, and the Kremlin regiment be enough?

And I whisper to myself, softly, beneath the singing of the choir:

"No."

Our repast in the White Chamber is quite ordinary today.

We sit at long, bare, oak tables. The servants bring us kvass made from bread crumbs, day-old cabbage soup, rye bread, beef boiled with onion, and buckwheat porridge. We eat, discuss our plans quietly. Our silent bells sway back and forth. Each *wing* of the oprichnina has its own plans: some are busy in the Secret Department today; some in the Mind Chamber; some in the Ambassadorial; some in the Trade Department. Right now I have three affairs going.

The first: deal with the clowns and minstrels, and approve the new performance for the holiday concert.

The second: snuff out *the star*.

The third: fly out and visit Praskovia, the clairvoyant of Tobol, on a special *errand*.

I sit in my place, the fourth to Batya's right. It's a place of honor, a lucrative place. Only Shelet, Samosya, and Yerokha are closer to him on the right side. Batya is strong, imposing, young in countenance, though completely gray. It's a pleasure to watch him eat: he doesn't hurry, he takes his time. Batya is our foundation, the main root of the oak that supports the entire oprichnina. He was the first to whom His Majesty entrusted the Work. During difficult, fateful times for Russia, our rulers leaned on him. Batya was the first link in the iron chain of the oprichniks. After him other links were attached, welded, fused into the Great Ring of the oprichnina, its sharp barbs pointed outward. With this ring His Majesty drew a sick, rotting, collapsing country together, he lassoed it like a wounded bear, dripping ichor blood. And the bear grew strong of bone and muscle, its wounds healed, it put on fat, its claws grew out. And we let its blood, blood that was rotten, poisoned by enemies. Now the roar of the Russian bear is heard by the entire world. Not only China and Europe, but lands beyond the ocean heed our roar.

I see Batya's mobilov blink red. Indirect conversations are forbidden during the repast. We all turn off our mobilovs. A red signal means His Majesty is calling. Batya puts his solid gold mobilov to his ear, and it jingles against his bell earring.

"At your service, Your Majesty."

Everyone in the refectory grows quiet. Batya's voice is the only sound:

"Yes, Your Majesty. I understand. We'll be there right away, Your Majesty."

Batya stands up, looks us over quickly:

"Vogul, Komiaga, Tiaglo, with me."

Ah. By Batya's voice I can sense something has happened. We stand, cross ourselves, and leave the refectory. By Batya's choice I understand—*an affair of the mind* awaits us. Everyone chosen has a university education. Vogul studied the workings of the treasury in St. Petrograd; Tiaglo specialized in book manufacturing in Nizhny Novgorod; and I joined the oprichnina from my third year at the history department of Moscow's Mikhailo Lomonosov State University. Actually, I didn't join . . . You don't join the oprichnina. You don't choose it. It chooses you. Or, more precisely, as Batya himself says when he's had a bit

to drink and snort: "The oprichnina pulls you in like a wave."
Oh, how it pulls you in! It pulls you in so fast that your head
spins, the blood in your veins boils, you see red stars. But that
wave can carry you out as well. It can carry you out in a minute,
irrevocably. This is worse than death. Falling out of the oprichnina is like losing both your legs. For the rest of your life you
won't be able to walk, only to crawl . . .

We go out in the yard. From the White Chamber to His
Majesty's Red Palace is just a stone's throw. But Batya turns
toward our Mercedovs. So that means we're not going to chat
in the Kremlin. We all get into our cars. Batya's Mercedov is
distinguished—wide, bug-eyed, squat, with glass three fingers
thick. It's high quality work by Chinese masters, custom-made
on special order, what they call *te tzo dei*. On the front hood is
the head of a German shepherd, on the back a steel broom. Batya
drives toward Savior Gates. We fall in line behind him and drive
out through a cordon of Streltsy. We cross Red Square. Today is
a market day; peddlers take up most of the square. The hawkers
shout, *saloop* men whistle, bread sellers boom, the Chinese sing.
The weather is sunny, nippy; there was a good snow during the
night. The main square of our country is cheerful, musical. As a
boy I witnessed an entirely different Red Square—grim, stern,
frightening, with a big pile of granite housing the corpse of the
Red Revolt's maker. At that time a cemetery of his henchmen
stood nearby. A gloomy picture. But His Majesty, our little
father, tore down the granite box, buried the corpse of the
squint-eyed rebel in the ground, and demolished the cemetery.
Then he ordered the Kremlin walls to be painted white. And the
main square of the country became genuinely *krasny*—red as in
krasivo, beautiful. And thank God. → making fun of Putin
tearing down comm + revival of orthodoxy

We drive toward the Hotel Moscow, along Mokhovaya
Street, past the National Hotel, past the Bolshoi and Maly the-
aters, past the Metropol Hotel, and onto Lubianskaya Square.

That's what I thought: the conversation will take place in the Secret Department. We drive around the square past the monument to Malyuta Skuratov. Our forefather stands there in bronze, dusted with snow, short, stocky, stooping, with long arms; he gazes intently from under overhanging eyebrows. For centuries he has watched over Moscow with the Ever-Watchful Eye of the State; he watches us, the heirs of the oprichniks' Great Work. He watches silently.

We drive up to the left gates; Batya honks. The gates open, and we enter the inner courtyard, park, and get out of our Mercedovs. We enter the Secret Department. Each time I walk under its gray marble arches, with their torches and stern crosses, my heart skips and then starts to beat differently. It's an out-of-the-ordinary, special beat. The beat of the state's Secret Work.

A dashing, fit lieutenant in a light blue uniform greets us and salutes. He accompanies us to the elevators, which carry us to the topmost floor, to the office of Terenty Bogdanovich Buturlin, the head of the Secret Department, a prince, and a close friend of His Majesty. We enter the office—first Batya, then the rest of us. Buturlin greets us. He and Batya shake hands; we bow to our waists. Buturlin's expression is serious. He shows Batya to a chair, and sits down across from him. We stand behind Batya. The head of the Secret Department has a menacing face. Terenty Bogdanovich is no joker. He loves to monitor important, complex, critical state affairs, to uncover and undermine conspiracies, catch traitors and spies, smash subversive plots. He sits silently, looking at us, fingering his carved bone beads. Then he says one word:

"Pasquinade."

Batya waits. We freeze and don't even breathe. Buturlin looks at us searchingly, and adds:

"On His Majesty's family."

Batya turns in the leather armchair, frowns, and cracks his large knuckles. We stand absolutely still. Buturlin gives a command, and the blinds on the office windows are lowered. A kind of twilight fills the room. The head of the Secret Department gives another command. Words are pulled up from the Russian Network; they hang in the dim light. The letters are iridescent, burning in the dark:

by Well-Meaning Anonymous
WEREWOLF AT A FIRE

Firemen are looking,
The police are looking,
Even priests are looking
Through our capital city.
They're seeking a Count,
Whom they haven't yet found,
Nor ever have seen,
A Count round about age thirty-three.

Of medium height,
Pensive and glum,
He's smartly attired,
In tails and cummerbund.
Cut in the signet ring
On his finger,
A hedgehog of diamond gleams and glims,
But not a whit more is known about him.

Nowadays,
Counts are oft
Pensive and glum,

Stylishly garbed,
In tails and cummerbund.
They adore the alluring
Dazzle of diamonds,
The *dolce vita*
Is just waiting to find them.

Who is he?
Whencesoever?
What manner of beast
The count whom they seek
In our
Capital city?
What hath he done,
This chic aristocrat?
Here's what Moscow's salons
Say to that!

Once, a Rolls-Royce
Wound its way,
All round Moscow.
A Count most forlorn,
Who resembled an owl,
Rode in it alone.
Sullenly squinting, morosely he yawned,
While humming an air
from a Wagner song.

All of a sudden,
In a glass 'cross the lane,
The Count
Spied a Marquess,
Encircled by flame.

A swarm of idlers,
Crowded the pavement,
The ancestral mansion
Was fully ablaze.
Gloating, the loafers
Ogled fire and pitch,
After all, such abodes
Were just for the rich.

Out of the cozy Rolls-Royce
The Count raced.
Ne'er a moment he wasted,
He cut through the rabble,
Of miserable swine,
Making very good time,
Then up, up, up,
Up the drainpipe
He climbed.

The third floor,
The fourth,
The fifth . . .
Then the last one,
Engulfed by the fire.
Out came piteous cries,
Then moans growing fainter—
Flames were now licking
The balcony sides.

Pale and quite naked,
Framed by the window,
The Marquess fluttered
In fantastical plumes;

Then a flare of the fire,
'Midst the dove-colored fumes,
Did illumine her milky white breast
On the pyre.

His hands strong and lithe,
The Count drew himself up,
Then with all of his might,
Slammed his brow
'Gainst the glass.
It shattered; shards took flight,
And lo! This remarkable sight,
Was met with but silence below.

One blow, another—
The window frame shuddered;
He stubbornly
Smashed the sash,
And crawled through the window,
Ripping his frock coat.
The idlers below whispered:
"Idiot . . . Ass . . ."

Then, in the window,
He appeared, stood up straight,
And embraced the young Marquess—
To his dickey he pressed her;
Above them smoke swirled,
Black, gray, and brindled,
Tongues of red fire,
Flickered and kindled.
The Count moaned

As he lowered his lips
To the breasts,
That he gripped in his hands.
The mob smirked with malice,
Spectators took note,
As a monstrous phallus
Arose in the smoke!

Onlookers gazed,
From way down below,
They saw the Count shudder,
As he entered the Marquess,
They glimpsed the pair quake,
And pull back from the window,
And then she and the Count
Disappeared in the haze!

A cloud of dust whirled,
And mingled with ash,
The firemen's cars sped
Hither and yon,
The rabble stepped back,
The police blew their whistles,
The firemen's helmets
Shone in the sun.

In the blink of an eye,
Copper helmets spread out;
Ladders reached higher and higher.
Fearless and brave,
One after the other,
Those fellows in Teflon

Climbed up and straight on
Through smoke and the fire.

The flames were replaced
By poisonous fumes,
From the pump water gushed
In a powerful stream.
An elderly servant,
Ran up to the firemen,
"Brothers, please save my lady, my queen!"

"Sorry," replied
The firemen affably,
"No lady was found
In this mansion!
We looked through and through,
We searched with great care;
Your beloved young Marquess
Was not anywhere!"

The old man sobbed,
And tore at his whiskers,
People gaped
At the balcony black.
Then out of the blue,
A dog's abrupt yelp,
Turned to a
Mournful whimper for help.

The crowd looked back and gawked.
Speeding off, the Rolls-Royce
Had run over a dog.

As its windows whizzed by,
a dim profile was glimpsed,
And silently faded,
Eclipsed by the glint,
Of a diamond hedgehog!

The mob on the sidewalk
Stood still, transfixed.
People followed
The Rolls-Royce's trail—
In the distance, the posh
Limousine drove off,
To the splatter of
Sputtering wheels.

Firemen are looking,
The Police are looking,
Even priests are looking
Through our capital city,
They're seeking a Count
Whom they never have seen,
A particular Count
About age thirty-three.

And you, gentlemen of the Malachite Chamber,
This werewolf you haven't chanced to encounter?

The last line fades. The subversive poem disappears, melts in the dark air. The blinds are raised. Buturlin sits silently. His brown eyes are focused on Batya, who glances at us. The target of this pasquinade is as clear as day. By our eyes Batya can tell that there isn't any doubt: the gloomy count with the diamond hedgehog carved in his ring is none other than Count Andrei Vladimirovich Urusov, His Majesty's son-in-law, professor of jurisprudence, an active member of the Russian Academy of Sciences, honorary chair of the Mind Department, chairman of the All-Russian Equine Society, chairman of the Association to Promote Air Flight, chairman of the Society of Russian Fisticuffs, comrade of the chairman of the Eastern Treasury, owner of the Southern Port, owner of the Izmailovsky and Donskoi markets, owner of the Moscow Association of Building Contractors, owner of the Moscow Brick Factory, co-owner of the Western Railroad. And the hint about the Malachite Chamber was also obvious: this new space, located under the Kremlin Concert Hall, was built for the rest and relaxation of the Inner Circle and their retinue. It's new, therefore *fashionable*. For that matter, the construction of the Malachite Chamber elicited quite a few subversive questions. Yes, yes, there were opponents . . .

"Is that clear, oprichniks?" Buturlin asks.

"Clear as a bell, Prince," Batya answers.

"There's just one little problem: find the author of the pasquinade."

Batya nods. "We'll track that worm down, he won't get away."

And, thoughtfully pulling on his short beard, he asks: "Does His Majesty know?"

"He knows," sounds a majestic voice, and we all bow low, touching the parquet with our right hands.

The sovereign face appears in the air of the office. Out of the corner of my eye I notice the iridescent gold frame around the beloved, narrow face with dark blond beard and thin mustache. We straighten up. His Majesty looks at us with his expressive, sincere intent and penetrating blue-gray eyes. His look is inimitable. You'd never confuse him with anyone else. And I am ready without hesitation to give my life for this look.

"I read it, I read it," says His Majesty. "It's artfully written."

"Your Majesty, we'll find the pasquinader, I assure you," says Buturlin.

"I don't doubt it. Although I have to admit that's not what concerns me, Terenty Bogdanovich."

"What concerns you, Your Majesty?"

"My dear, I'm concerned about whether or not everything written in the poem . . . is true."

"What specifically, Your Majesty?"

"All of it."

Buturlin grows thoughtful.

"Your Majesty, I find that difficult to answer immediately. Permit me to take a look at the report of the Fire Department council."

"Come now, you don't need any fire reports, Prince." His Majesty's transparent eyes look straight through Buturlin. "You need witnesses to the event."

"Who do you have in mind, Your Majesty?"

"The hero of the poem."

Buturlin looks at Batya, who is gritting his teeth.

"Your Majesty, we do not have the right to question members of your family," says Batya.

"And I'm not forcing you to interrogate anyone. I simply want to know—is it all true?"

Silence again fills the office. The shining image of His Majesty glitters with gold and rainbow colors.

Our sire grins. "Why so quiet now? It won't work without me?"

"Without you, Your Majesty, nothing works," says Buturlin, bowing his head so low that his bald spot shows.

"All right then, we'll do it your way." His Majesty sighs. In a loud voice he calls:

"Andrei!"

About fifteen seconds pass, and to the right of His Majesty's face a small picture of Count Urusov appears in a violet frame. By the count's grave, haggard look it is clear that he has read the poem—more than once.

"Good day, Father." The count bows his large, big-eared head, which sits on a short neck; his brow is narrow and he has large facial features; his chestnut hair is thin.

"Hello, hello, son-in-law." The gray-blue eyes look at him with absolute calm. "Read this poem about yourself?"

"I've read it, Father."

"Not badly written, don't you think? And here my academicians go on and on about how we don't have any good poets!"

Count Urusov keeps quiet, pursing his thin lips. His mouth, like a frog's, is extremely wide.

"Tell us, Andrei, is it true?"

The count says nothing, casts his eyes down, inhales, sniffs, and exhales carefully:

"It's true, Your Majesty."

Now His Majesty himself grows thoughtful, and frowns. We all stand there, waiting.

"So you mean to say that you actually like to fornicate at fires?" asks His Majesty.

The count nods his grave head:

"It's true, Your Majesty."

"Hmmm. That's how it is, hey? . . . Rumors had reached me before this, but I didn't believe them. I thought that envious people were slandering you. But you . . . Hmm, so that's what you are."

"Your Majesty, I can explain everything—"

"When did this start?"

"Your Majesty, I swear to you in the name of all the saints, I swear on my mother's grave—"

"Don't swear," His Majesty says suddenly, and in *such* a voice that all of us feel our hair stand up.

It isn't a shout, and he isn't grinding his teeth, but it has the effect of red-hot tongs. His Majesty's fury is terrifying. And even more terrifying because our sire never raises his voice.

Count Urusov is no coward—he's a statesman, a wheeler-dealer, a millionaire of millionaires, an inveterate hunter who goes after bears with nothing but a spear out of *principle*—but even he pales before this voice, like some second-year high school student called to the principal's office.

"Tell me, when did you first indulge in this vice?"

The count licks his dry, froglike lips.

"Your Majesty, it . . . it was completely by accident . . . even really, you know . . . as though I were being forced. Although, of course, I'm guilty . . . only I . . . I . . . it's my sin, mine, forgive me."

"Explain everything in order."

"I'll tell you, I'll tell you everything, I won't hide anything at all. Once, when I was seventeen years old, I was walking along Ordynka Street and I saw a house on fire, and there was a woman crying out. The firemen hadn't gotten there yet. People gave me a boost up, I climbed in the window to help her. She threw herself on my chest . . . Your Majesty, I don't know what overcame me . . . I must have blanked out . . . and, well, the woman, wasn't exactly a beauty to put it mildly, medium height . . . well, and . . . I . . . you see . . ."

"And?"

"Well, I had her, Your Majesty. They were barely able to pull us out of the flames later on. After that, I wasn't myself anymore. I kept thinking and thinking about the incident . . . A month later I was in St. Petrograd—I was walking along Liteiny—and there was an apartment burning on the third floor. That time my legs just led me there—I broke down the door—I don't know where I got the strength. And inside there was a mother with her child. She was pressing him to her breast, and screaming out the window. Well, I took her from behind . . . And then six months later in Samara the treasury burned down, and my deceased father and I had come for the market, and then . . ."

"That's enough. Whose house burned the last time?"

"Princess Bobrinskaya's."

"Why does this rhymester call a Russian princess a 'marquess'?"

"I don't know, Your Majesty . . . Probably out of hatred for Russia."

"All right. Now tell me honestly . . . did you set that house on fire deliberately?"

The count freezes as though he's just been bitten by a snake. He lowers his lynxlike eyes. And says nothing.

"I'm asking you—did you set that house on fire?"

The count heaves a painful sigh:

"I cannot lie to you, Your Majesty. I set it on fire."

His Majesty is silent for a moment. Then he says:

"It is not for to me to judge your vice—each of us will answer to God for these things. But I cannot forgive arson. Get out of here!"

Urusov's face disappears. The four of us remain alone with His Majesty. His brow is creased with sadness.

"Hmmm . . . well." His Majesty sighs. "And I entrusted my daughter to a swine like that."

We remain silent.

"So that's it, Prince," His Majesty continues. "It's a family affair. I'll deal with him myself."

"As you command, Your Majesty. And what about the pasquinader?"

"Act according to the law. On second thought . . . don't. It could arouse unhealthy curiosity. Simply tell him not to write anything like that again."

"Yes, sir."

"Thank you all for your service."

"We serve the Fatherland!" we say as we bow. *? No longer "motherland?"*

His Majesty's image disappears. We look at one another in relief. Buturlin paces the office, shaking his head:

"That cad, Urusov . . . shame on him!"

"Thank God that we don't have to deal with that mess," says Batya, smoothing his beard. "But who is the author?"

"We'll find out right now," says Buturlin. He walks over to his desk and sits in his work chair. His voice commands:

"Writers—come here!"

Immediately the faces of 128 writers appear in the air of the office. They are all framed in stern brown and arranged in a neat square. Three enlarged faces float over the rest: the gray-haired chairman of the Writers' Chamber, Pavel Olegov, with a continually suffering expression on his puffy face, and two even grayer, gloomier, anxious deputies, Anany Memzer and Pavlo Basinya. By the doleful expression on all three mugs, I realize that a difficult conversation awaits them.

"We'll leave, Terenty Bogdanovich," Batya says, reaching out to shake hands with the prince. "Writers are your bailiwick."

"All the best, Boris Borisovich." Buturlin shakes Batya's hand.

We bow to the prince and follow Batya out. We walk along the hallway to an elevator, accompanied by the same dashing officer.

"Listen, Komiaga, how come Olegov is always such a sour puss? What is it—toothache?" Batya asks me.

"His soul aches, Batya. For Russia."

"Ah, that's good." Batya nods. "And what's he written? You know I'm not one for books."

"*The Russian Tile Oven in the Twenty-first Century*. A weighty piece. I didn't get all the way through it . . ."

"The Russian oven . . . that's wonderful . . ." Batya sighs thoughtfully. "Especially when you bake liver pies . . . Where are you off to now?"

"To the Kremlin Concert Hall."

"Right," he said, nodding. "See you sort that one out. Those clowns are up to something new . . ."

I nod in reply. "We'll sort it out, Batya."

The Kremlin Concert Hall has always delighted me. It thrilled me when I first visited it with my deceased parents twenty-six years ago, to see *Swan Lake*; when I ate blini with red caviar during the intermission; when I called my friend Pashka on Papa's mobilov from the buffet; when I peed in the spacious toilet; when I watched the mysterious ballerinas in snow white tutus; and even now, when my temples are sprinkled with their first gray.

A magnificent hall! Everything in it is grand, it has all the amenities for state holidays, everything is perfect. Only one thing is wrong—not all the events produced on this mighty stage are appropriate. Subversiveness seeps through even here. Well, that's why we exist, to keep order and exterminate rebellion.

We sit in the empty hall. On my right is the director. On my left, an observer from the Secret Department. In front of me is Prince Sobakin of the Inner Circle. Behind me—the head of the Culture Chamber. Serious people, state servants. We're watching the holiday concert that's coming up. It begins powerfully, like a peal of thunder: a song about His Majesty shakes the dimly lit hall. The Kremlin choir sings well. Russia knows how to sing. Especially if the song is from the soul.

The song ends; the valiant fellows in decorated shirts bow, the girls in *sarafans* and holiday headdresses curtsey. Sheaves of grain bow in an iridescent rainbow, and above them frozen river willows bow. Natural sunlight shines, almost blindingly. Good. I approve. All the others approve as well. The long-haired director is happy.

The next song is about Russia. No questions here, either. It's a strong piece, finely polished. Next—an historical number: the time of Ivan III. A grim, fateful time in Russian history. A serious struggle for the integrity of the Russian state is under way— a fledgling state, not yet strong, only beginning to stand on its own. There's thunder and lightning on stage, Ivan's warriors are heading for the breach, the Metropolitan raises a cross illumined by flickering flames. Rebellious Novgorod, which opposes the unification of Russia, is conquered; the apostates fall on their knees, but Great Prince Ivan Vasilevich's sword touches their guilty heads with mercy:

"Neither enemie nor adversary be I. I am Protector, Father, and Defender of you and all the Great Russian Kingdom."

Bells ring. A rainbow shines above Novgorod and over all of Rus. The heavenly birds sing. The Novgorodians bow and sob with joy.

Now, that's good, that's appropriate. But the warriors should have broader shoulders and the Metropolitan could be taller, more dignified. And there's a good deal of unnecessary fuss in the background. The birds fly too low, they're distracting. The director agrees with the suggestions, and makes notes in his book.

The next act is a page from our recent past, troubled and sad. Three Stations Square in Moscow, during the years of the accursed White Revolt. Simple people mill about, brought out of their homes onto the square by a wave of rebellion, forced to sell whatever comes to hand to earn enough for a piece of bread, stolen from them by criminal rulers. My earliest childhood memories are of those *foul* times. The Time of the White Pus, which poisoned our Russian bear . . . back when the inhabitants of Russia stood on the square with teakettles, frying pans, shirts, even shampoo and soap in their hands. Refugees and people who had lost everything flooded into Moscow and traveled there from grief. Elderly men, the war-wounded, veterans and heroes of labor. Seeing that crowd left a bitter taste indeed. The sky above is overcast and dank. Sad music sounds from the orchestra pit. Then, as though a pale ray of hope has suddenly pierced the gloomy picture, the colors of center stage grow warmer and we see three homeless children, rejected by the world: two little girls in torn dresses and a grimy little boy holding a teddy bear. The timid flute of hope comes alive, awakes and sounds, striving upward with its delicate voice. Over the gloomy, sullied square we hear a touching children's song:

"I hear a voice arising, lovely in the distance—
The voice of dawn, adorned in silver dew.
I hear a voice, and now the road, insistent,
Does daze me like the childhood swings that I once knew.

"O distance lovely, don't be cruel.
Do not be cruel, oh cruel never be!
From purest streams to lovely distance
The road to lovely distance beckons me.

"I hear a voice arising in the distance,
It summons me to far and marv'lous climes.
I hear a voice; it asks of me, insistent,
What deed I've done today to aid tomorrow's time.

"O distance lovely, don't be cruel.
Do not be cruel, oh cruel never be!
From purest streams to lovely distance,
The road to lovely distance beckons me."

Tears well up in my eyes. It's the *hangover*, of course. But the dignified Prince Sobakin is sniffing as well. He has a large family, many small grandchildren. The brawny observer from the Secret Department sits still as a statue. Well, of course—they have nerves of steel, they're ready for anything and everything. The portly head of the Culture Chamber sort of shakes his shoulders like he's caught a chill—he seems to be fighting off tears, too. The piece hits a raw nerve even in strong, seasoned men. That's wonderful . . .

His Majesty awakened in us not simply pride in our country, but compassion for her painful past. Three Russian children stand stretching their hands out to us from the past of an insulted and injured country. And we cannot help them at all.

We approve it.

Next—the present day. A full, bountiful cup. The Moiseev Ensemble performs dances of all the peoples of Great Russia. Here you've got the smooth Tatar dances, and the dashing Cossack whirls with sabers drawn; Tambov quadrilles to the sound of an accordion; and Nizhny Novgorod folk dances with their rattles and whistles; the whooping, yelping Chechen circle dance; Yakut tambourines; and the Chukots with their Arctic fox furs; the Kariaksky deer; the Kalmyk rams; Jewish frock coats—and Russian, Russian, Russian dancing till you drop—dashing, boisterous, bonding, reconciling everyone.

No question about this legendary group.

There are two more acts: "Flying Balalaikas," and "A Young Girl Rushes to a Rendezvous." Now these are real classics—everything honed, checked, polished. A feast for the eyes. You watch, and it's just like you're sledding down a hill. The observer applauds. We do, too. Good for His Majesty's artistes!

Then comes a short literary piece: "Hello, My Dear Nanny, Arina Rodionovna!" It's a little old, a bit forced. But the people love it and His Majesty respects it. The head of the Culture Chamber suggests lamely that Pushkin should be younger—the same not-very-young actor, Khapensky, has been playing the poet for the last twelve years. But we all know it's pointless. The actor is one of Her Highness's favorites. The director shrugs his shoulders, opens his hands:

"Gentlemen, you must understand, it's not up to me . . ."

We understand.

And now we come to the most important act. A new piece on the topic of the day: "Like Hell I Will!"

Each of us squirms in his seat and tenses. The stage is dark, the only sounds are the howl of the wind, and the strumming of the Kazakh dombra and the Russian balalaika. The moon crawls out from behind clouds, illuminating the scene with a faint light. In the middle of the stage is the Third Western Pipeline. The very one that's caused so much hullabaloo the last year and a half, so much trouble and concern. The pipeline stretches across the stage, through Russian forest and field; sparkling in the dim light, it arrives at the Western Wall. There it passes through a flow-regulating valve marked closed, dives into the wall, and moves farther westward. Our border guard stands there with an automatic ray gun, looking through binoculars toward the other side. Suddenly the dombras and balalaikas grow anxious, a warning bass sounds—and near the valve a molehill erupts. In a flash, a mole-saboteur in black goggles crawls out, looks around, sniffs the air, jumps, grabs the valve, digs his huge teeth into it with all his might. He's just about to turn it, to let the gas through. But—a ravaging ray flashes from the wall and cuts the mole in half! The mole's guts tumble out, a howl rends the air, and the thieving saboteur breathes his last. Lights flare, and three bold border guards, full of mettle, leap from the wall. Their jumps are agile, accompanied by handsprings and valiant whistles. One of them holds an accordion, the second a tambourine, the third wields wooden spoons. Each of them wears an automatic, loyal and true, on his back. The fine young border guards sing:

"The valves we closed up:
Like His Majesty told us.
But fiendish foes did try
To suck our gas completely dry.

"Right off we told them: 'No! We'll fight!'
And honed our eagle gaze.
Europa Gas, that parasite,
For Russian gas must pay!

"Just try to stop those cyberpunksters,
Across the wall's most chilly side.
What bifurcations, made by funksters,
Like mushrooms sprout both far and wide.

"Each time more brazen do they act,
But wait a moment, contemplate,
How could we give them gas like that?
In a thrice they'd suffocate."

One border guard opens the valve while the two others rush to the end of the pipe, put it to their rear ends, and fart. With a menacing howl the good fellows' farts pass through the pipe, flow through the wall, and . . . screams and wailing are heard in the West. The final chord sounds, and the three valiant fellows jump onto the pipe, raising their automatics in victory. Curtain.

The high-placed audience stirs. They're looking at Prince Sobakin. He twists his mustache, thinking. He speaks:

"Well now, what opinions do we have, gentlemen?"

The head of the Culture Chamber speaks:

"I see an obvious element of obscenity. Although the piece is topical and executed with vim and vigor."

The observer from the Secret Department:

"First of all, I don't like the enemy scout being killed rather than captured alive. Second, why only three border guards? I know for a fact that outposts have a dozen. So there should be twelve guards. Then the fart itself would be more powerful . . ."

I:

"I agree in regard to the composition of the border guard. And this is a much-needed number, a topical number. But there is an element of obscenity. And His Majesty, as we all know, champions chastity and cleanliness on stage."

Prince Sobakin says nothing, but nods. Then he speaks:

"Tell me, gentlemen, does hydrogen sulfide, which our valiant warriors fart—does it burn?"

The observer nods. "It burns."

"Well, if it burns," the prince continues, twisting his mustached, "then what does Europe have to fear from our farts?"

Now that's a member of the Inner Circle for you! He sees right to the bottom of things! You can heat European cities with Russian farts! Everyone grows thoughtful. I blame my brain: I didn't catch on to an obvious thing! But then, my education was in the humanities . . .

The director pales and coughs nervously.

The observer scratches his beard. "Hmm. Yes . . . there's a little discrepancy . . ."

"A blunder in the script!" The culture head lifts a fat finger in forewarning. "Who's the author?"

In the darkness of the hall a lean man in glasses and a belted peasant shirt appears.

"My good man, how did you slip up like this? The story of our gas is as old as the world!" the culture head asks him.

"I'm at fault. I'll fix it."

"Fix it, fix it, my dear," yawns the prince.

"Just remember that dress rehearsal is the day after tomorrow!" the observer says sternly.

"We'll make it in time, of course."

"One more thing," the prince adds. "On the subject of moles: the ray gun causes his intestines to fall out. It's a bit too much."

"What, your Highness?"

"Intestines. Naturalism is out of place here. Fewer gizzards, my man."

"At your command. We'll fix everything."

"And what about the obscenity?" I ask.

The prince glances at me sideways:

"It isn't obscenity, Sir Oprichnik, but healthy army humor, which helps our Streltsy bear the severe conditions on the far borders of our Motherland."

Laconic. Can't argue. The prince is smart. And judging by his cold, sideways look—he doesn't like us oprichniks. Well, that's understandable: we step on the Inner Circle's toes, we breathe down their necks.

"What else is there?" the prince asks, taking out a nail file.

"The aria of Ivan Susanin."

Don't have to watch that one. I rise, bow, and head toward the exit. Suddenly in the darkness someone grabs me by the hand:

"Sir, Sir Oprichnik, I beg of you!"

A woman.

"Who are you?" I pull my hand away.

"I beg of you, hear me out!" she says in a hot, fitful whisper. "I'm the wife of the arrested scribe Koretsky."

"Get away, you Zemstvo spawn."

"I beg you, I beg of you!" She falls on her knees and grabs my legs.

"Away with you." I kick her in the chest with my boot.

She lies on the floor. Then, from behind me—another pair of hot female hands, and more whispering:

"Andrei Danilovich, we beg you, beg you!"

I grab my dagger from its scabbard:

"Away, you whores!"

Thin hands recoil in the darkness:

"Andrei Danilovich, I am not a whore. I am Uliana Sergeevna Kozlova."

Ah! The prima ballerina of the Bolshoi Theatre. His Majesty's favorite, the best Odile and Giselle of all . . . I didn't recognize her in the dark. I look closer. Yes—it's her. And the Zemstvo bitch lies prone. I remove my dagger:

"Madame, how may I be of service?"

Kozlova comes closer. Her face, like the faces of all ballerinas, is far more ordinary than on stage. And she's not in the least tall.

"Andrei Danilovich," she whispers, glancing at the dim stage, where Susanin, with his stick and sheepskin coat, sings his aria slowly, "I beseech you to intercede, I implore you in the name of all the saints, I beg you with my heart! Klavdia Lvovna is the godmother of my children, she's my closest, most beloved friend, she's an honest, pure, God-fearing woman, together we built a school for orphans, an orphanage, a neat, spacious school, where orphans study. I beg of you, we beg of you . . . the day after tomorrow Klavdia Lvovna will be sent to the settlement, there's only a day left, I beseech you as a Christian, as a man, as a theatergoer, as a cultured person, we will be in your eternal debt, we will pray for you and for your family, Andrei Danilovich—"

"I don't have a family," I interrupt.

She looks at me silently with large, moist eyes. Susanin sings "My time has come!" and crosses himself. The Zemstvo widow lies on the floor. I ask:

"Why are you, a favorite of His Majesty's family, asking me?"

"His Majesty is terribly angry at the former chairman and all of his assistants. He doesn't want to hear anything about clemency. But the clerk Koretsky personally wrote that very letter to the French. His Majesty doesn't want to hear a word about the Koretskys."

"All the more . . . What can I do?"

"Andrei Danilovich, the oprichnina is capable of miracles."

"Madame, the oprichnina creates the Work and Word! of the state."

"You are one of the leaders of that mighty order."

"Madame, the oprichnina is not an order, but a brotherhood."

"Andrei Danilovich! I beseech you! Take pity on an unfortunate woman. In your masculine wars we are the ones who suffer most. And life on earth depends on us."

Her voice trembles. The Zemstvo woman's sobs are barely audible behind her. The culture head glances sideways in our direction. What can you do, people ask us to intercede almost every day. But Koretsky and that whole gang of the Public Chambers chairman—they are double-dealers! Better not to even look their way.

"Tell her to leave," I say.

"Klavdia Lvovna, dear heart . . ." The ballerina leans over her. Koretskaya disappears in the dark, sobbing.

"Let's go outside." I head toward the door with the illuminated word "Exit."

Kozlova hurries after me. Silently, we leave the building through the service entrance.

On the square I go to my Mercedov. Kozlova follows me. In daylight the best Giselle in Russia is even more frail and plain. She hides her thin little face in a luxurious arctic fox collar with a short throat wrap. The prima ballerina wears a long, narrow skirt of black silk; under it, pointed black boots with patches of snakeskin peek out. The prima has beautiful eyes—large, gray, anxious.

"If it's uncomfortable for you, we can speak in my car." She nods in the direction of a lilac-colored Cadillac.

"Better in mine." I show my palm to the Mercedov and it obediently opens its glass top.

Even tax collectors don't make deals in other people's cars these days. A seedy scrivener from the Trade Department would never sit down in someone else's car to talk about a *black* petition.

I take my place. She sits to my right in the only seat.

"We'll take a ride, Uliana Sergeevna," I say as I start the engine, and drive out of the government parking lot.

"Andrei Danilovich, I've been in worried to death all week long . . ." She takes out a pack of women's Motherland and lights up. "There's a sense of doom around this affair. It turns out that I can't do anything to help my oldest friend. And I have a performance tomorrow."

"She's truly dear to you?"

"Terribly. I don't have any other girlfriends. You know the ways of our theater world . . ."

"I've heard about it." I drive out of the Borovitsky Gates, turn onto the Great Stone Bridge, and speed down the red lane.

Taking a drag on her cigarette, Kozlova looks at the White-stone Kremlin and the barely distinguishable snow on it.

"You know, I was very anxious before meeting you."

"Why?"

"I never thought that asking for others would be so difficult."

"I agree."

"And then . . . last night I had a strange dream: the black bands were still on the main cupola of Uspensky Cathedral and His Majesty was still in mourning for his first wife."

"Did you know Anastasia Fyodorovna?"

"No. I wasn't a prima ballerina at the time."

We reach Yakimanka Street. The Zamoskvoreche neighborhood is noisy and crowded as usual.

"So, I can count on your help?"

"I'm not promising anything, but I can try."

"How much will it cost?"

"There are standard prices. Zemstvo affairs currently cost a thousand in gold. Departmental—three thousand. But an affair in the Public Chambers . . ."

"But I'm not asking you to close the case. I'm asking for the widow!"

I slow down as I drive down Ordynka Street. Good Lord, how many Chinese there are here . . .

"Andrei Danilovich! Don't torture me!"

"Well . . . for you . . . two and a half. And an aquarium."

"What kind?"

"Well, not a silver one!" I grin.

"When?"

"If they're sending your friend off the day after tomorrow, then the sooner the better."

"So, today?"

"You've got the right idea."

"All right. Please drive me home, if it's not too much trouble. I'll get my car later . . . I live on Nezhdanov Street."

I turn around and race back.

"Andrei Danilovich, what kind of money will you need?"

"Preferably gold pieces of the second minting."

"All right. I think I'll be able to get the money together by evening. But the aquarium . . . You know, I don't do gold aquariums; we ballerinas aren't paid as much as it seems . . . But Lyosha Voroniansky is *sitting* on piles of gold. He's a great friend of mine. I'll get it from him."

Voroniansky is the premier tenor of the Bolshoi Opera, the people's idol. He not only *sits* on gold, he probably eats off it . . . I zip across the Great Stone Bridge again, in the red lane. On my right and left cars sit in endless traffic jams. After the Nestor Public Library I pass Vozdvizhenka Street, the university, and turn onto disgraced Nikitskaya Street. The third cleaning has passed and the street has quieted down. Here, even the hawkers and bread peddlers walk fearfully and their cries are timid. The windows of burned-out apartments that have never been restored blacken menacingly. The Zemstvo swine are scared. And for good reason . . .

I turn onto Nezhdanov Street and stop near the gray artists' building. It's fenced off by a three-meter-high wall with a constant ray of light shining upward. That's all as it should be . . .

"Wait for me, Andrei Danilovich," says the prima ballerina as she gets out of the car. She disappears into the lobby.

I call Batya:

"Batya, we've got a request for a half-deal."

"Who is it?"

"The clerk Koretsky."

"Who's buying?"

"Kozlova."

"The ballerina?"

"That's right. Do we help the widow beat the rap?"

"We can try. We'll have to share quite a bit to manage it. When's the money?"

"She'll have it by evening. And . . . my heart can feel it, Batya, she's going to bring an aquarium out to me shortly."

"That's great." Batya winks at me. "If she does—drive straight to the baths."

"You bet!"

Kozlova is taking a long time. I light a cigarette. I turn on the *clean* teleradio. It allows us to see and hear what our domestic dissenters spend so much time and energy to listen to and watch at night. First I go through the underground: the Free Settlements channel broadcasts lists of people arrested the previous night, and talks about the "true story" behind the Kunitsyn affair. Fools! Who's persuaded by these "true stories"? . . . Radio Hope is quiet during the day—they're catching up on sleep, those late-night SOBs. But the Siberian River Pirate, the voice of runaway prisoners, is wide awake:

"At the request of 2ován, Poltorá-Iván, released just three days ago, we'll play an old convict song."

A juicy harmonica starts, and a husky young voice sings:

"Two convicts lay flat on their bunk beds
And dreamed of a past that they craved.
The first one was nicknamed Bacillus,
The other one's handle was Plague."

This River Pirate, jumping around western Siberia like a flea, has been caught between the nails twice: first the local Secret Department squashed it; then we did. They got away from the department guys, and they hopped away from us using Chinese aquariums. While negotiations over the ransom were going on, our guys managed to put three newscasters on the rack and dislocate their arms, and like a huge bear Sivolai knocked up the female announcer. But the backbone of the radio station remained whole; it bought a new, horse-drawn studio, and those shackle-fetters began broadcasting once again. Fortunately, His Majesty doesn't pay much attention to them. Why not let them yowl their prison songs?

"All Siberia howled in sync,
Their fame reached to old Kolymá.
Bacillus he fled the taigá,
While Plague returned to the clink."

I tune in to the West. It's the real stronghold of anti-Russian subversion. Like slimy reptiles in a cesspool, enemy voices teem: Freedom for Russia!, Voice of America, Free Europe, Freedom, the German Wave, Russia in Exile, Russian Rome, Russian Berlin, Russian Paris, Russian Brighton Beach, Russian Riviera.

I choose Freedom, the most vehement of the vermin, and I immediately run up against sedition, fresh out of the oven: they have an emigrant poet in the studio, a narrow-chested, dour-eyed Judas, an old acquaintance of ours with a shattered right hand (Poyarok made use of his foot during an interrogation). Straightening his old-fashioned glasses with his mutilated hand, the traitor reads in a quivering, nearly hysterical falsetto:

"Where there's a pair of Grafs—there's a paragraph!
Where there's just a court—no justice is courted!
You'll 'do your time,' without ever hearing 'time to go,'
Since by rights you're not arighted!"

The Judas! With a touch of my finger I remove the pale face of the liberal from my sight. These people are like unto vile worms that feed and nourish themselves on carrion. Spineless, twisted, insatiable, blind—that's why they are kindred with the despicable worm. Liberals differ from the lowly worm only in their mesmerizing, witch-brewed speechifying. Like venom and reeking puss they spew it all about, poisoning humans and God's very world, defiling its holy purity and simplicity, befouling it as far as the very bluest horizon of the heavenly vault with the reptilian drool of their mockery, jeers, derision, contempt, double-dealing, disbelief, distrust, envy, spite, and shamelessness.

Freedom for Russia! whines about "persecuted will," the Old Believers' "Posolon" grumbles about corruption in the top hierarchy of the Russian Orthodox Church; Russian Paris reads a book by Iosif Bak, *Hysterical Gesticulation as a Way to Survive in Contemporary Russia*; Russian Rome plays some kind of shrill monkeylike jazz; Russian Berlin broadcasts an ideological duel between two irreconcilable bastard-mongrel emigrants; the Voice of America has a program called "Russian Expletives in Exile" with an obscene retelling of the immortal work *Crime and Punishment*:

"The un-fucking-believable blow of the butt-fucking axe hit the goddamn temple of the triply gang-banged old bag, facilitated piss-perfectly by her cunt-sucking short height. She cried out cumly and suddenly collapsed on the jism-covered shit-paneled floor, although that rotten pussy-hole of a hag had time to raise both of her ass-licking hands to her fuckin' bare-ass pimped-up head."

An abomination. What else can be said?

Our liberals are dripping with anger and grinding their teeth after His Majesty's famous Decree 37, which criminalized obscene language in public and private, and made obligatory public corporal punishment the sentence. Most surprising of all is that our people immediately accepted Decree 37 with understanding. There were some show trials, some *drawing and quartering* on the main squares of Russian cities, the whistle of the cattle whip on Sennaya Square, and cries on the Manezh. And in a trice the people stopped using the filthy words that foreigners forced on them in bygone days. Only the intelligentsia has trouble coming to terms with it, and keeps on belching forth foul fumes in kitchens, bedrooms, latrines, elevators, storerooms, back streets, and cars, refusing to part with this putrid polyp on the body of the Russian language, which has poisoned more than one generation of our compatriots. And the loathsome West plays up to our underground foul-mouths.

The Russian Riviera dares—in a brazen, impudent tone—to criticize His Majesty's order to close the Third Western Pipeline for twenty-four hours. How much anger those European gentlemen have accumulated! For decades they have sucked our gas without thinking of the hardship it brought to our hardworking people. What astonishing news they report! Oh dear, it's cold in Nice *again*! Gentlemen, you'll have to get used to eating cold foie gras at least a couple of times a week. Bon appétit! China turned out to be smarter than you . . .

A knock and ring. That same clerk from the Ambassadorial Department:

"Andrei Danilovich, Korostylev here. The reception for the Albanian ambassador has been postponed until tomorrow at two o'clock."

"Got it." I turn off the clerk's owly mug.

Thank God, because today we're up to our ears in work. At state receptions for foreign accreditation, the oprichniks now stand next to the ambassadorials. Previously we alone carried the silver vessel holding the water. And a *dozen* ambassadorials stood in attendance in a half-circle. After August 17 His Majesty decided to bring them closer in. Now we hold the vessel jointly with the ambassadorials: Batya and Zhuravlev hold the cup; I, or someone from the right *wing*, holds the towel; the embassy clerk supports the elbow; and the rest stand on the rug or bow. As soon as His Majesty greets the new ambassador with a handshake and takes the credentials, we immediately begin the ritual washing of His Majesty's hands. Of course, it's a pity that the ambassadorials have been promoted after the mishaps of August. But—that is His Majesty's will . . .

Kozlova finally comes out.

By her eyes I can sense that she has it. I immediately feel a rush of blood, and my heart quickens.

"Andrei Danilovich." Through the window she hands me a plastic bag from a Chinese takeaway. "The money will be ready before six o'clock. I'll call."

I nod. Trying to restrain myself, I toss the bag casually onto the empty seat and close the window. Kozlova leaves. I drive off, turning onto Tverskaya Street. Near the Moscow Municipal Duma I park in the red lot for government cars. I stick my hand in the bag. My fingers touch the cool, smooth sphere. My fingers embrace it gently as I close my eyes: an *aquarium*! It's been a long time, oh so very long since my fingers have held the sublime globe. Almost four days. How terrible . . .

My hands sweaty from excitement, I take the globe out of the bag and place it in my left palm: there they are! Gold ones!

The ball is transparent, manufactured from the finest materials. It's filled with a clear, nourishing solution. In that solution swim seven tiny (only five millimeters each) gold sterlets. I look at them, bringing the ball close to my face. Teeny, tiny microscopic little fish! Divine, charming creatures. People of great intelligence created you for our pleasure. In ancient times, nimble golden fish like you, magical fish, brought happiness to Ivan Simpletons in the form of carved towers, tsars' daughters, and self-kindling Russian tile ovens. But the happiness that you bring, divine little ones, cannot be compared to any towers or self-kindling tile ovens, nor to women's caresses . . .

I look the globe over. Even without a magnifying glass I can see—Giselle did not deceive us! Seven gold sterlets in my hand. I take out the glass and gaze more intently: superb, obviously made in China, not in wretched America and definitely not in Holland. They frisk about in their native element, shining in the miserly Moscow winter sun. How glorious!

I call Batya. I show him the globe.

"Atta boy, Komiaga." Batya winks at me and in a sign of approval flicks his bell earring.

"Where to, Batya?"

"The Donskoi."

"I'm off!" I speed out of the parking lot.

On the way to the Donskoi Baths I try to figure out how to plan my work for the rest of the day and evening, how to get everything done. But my thoughts are muddled, I can't concentrate— the golden sterlets are right here, splashing in the sphere! Gritting my teeth, I force myself to think about state affairs. It seems I can manage everything—extinguish the *star*, and fly to see the soothsayer.

Donskoi Street is jam-packed. I turn on the State Snarl. A corps of cars quakes from the invisible sound, yields the road to me, pulling over. Great and powerful is the State Snarl. It clears the road like a bulldozer. I fly, I rush as to a fire. But the gold sterlet is more powerful than a fire! More powerful than an earthquake.

I whiz along to the yellow building of the Donskoi Baths. Outside, rising to the roof, is a figure of a bathhouse attendant with a broad, thick blond beard and two bunches of birch twigs in his muscular hand. The giant attendant thrashes his twigs and winks a mischievous blue eye every half-minute.

Holding the sphere tight in a deep pocket of my jacket, under my caftan, I enter. The doormen bow to their waist. *Our* room has already been reserved by Batya. I let them take my black caftan, and I continue down a vaulted corridor. My copper-soled boots clatter on the stone floor. Next to the door that leads to our room stands another attendant—strapping, tattooed Koliakha. He's an old acquaintance, who always watches out for the oprichniks' peace-of-mind time. A stranger could never get past broad-shouldered Koliakha.

"Greetings, Koliakha!" I say to him.

"To your health, Andrei Danilovich." He bows.

"Anyone else yet?"

"You are the first."

That's good. I'll choose the best place for myself.

Koliakha lets me into the room. It isn't very wide and has low ceilings. But it's cozy, familiar, lived in. In the middle is a round font, to the right is the steam room. It stands empty for want of use. For we now have *special* steam, ingenious steam. You couldn't find birch branches for it anywhere in the world . . .

The lounge chairs are arranged around the font like daisy petals. Seven. The number of fish in the sacred sphere. I fetch it from my brocade jacket pocket, and sit down on the edge of the chair. The sphere of fish lies in my palm. The golden sterlets romp in their element. Even without a magnifying glass, you can tell they're passing fair. An exceptional mind created this pleasure. Perhaps it wasn't human. Such a thing could be conceived only by angels falling from the Lord's throne.

I toss the sphere from palm to palm. Not an inexpensive pleasure. One sphere like this outweighs my monthly remuneration. It's a pity that these magical spheres are strictly forbidden in our Orthodox country. Not in ours alone, either. In America they give you ten years for silver fish, and about three times that for gold. In China they hang you straight off. And in putrefying Europe, these spheres are too hard to chew. Cyberpunks prefer cheap *acid*. For the last four years our Secret Department has been catching these fish. However, as always, they swim over to us from neighboring China. They swim and swim, passing through the border nets. And they'll keep on swimming.

To be honest, I don't see anything antigovernmental in these fish. Ordinary folk can't afford them, while the rich and those of high position must have their weaknesses; after all, weakness has many faces. In his time, His Majesty's father, Nikolai Platonovich, issued the great decree "On the Use of Energizing and Relaxing Remedies." This decree permitted the general use of *coke*, *angel dust*, and *weed* forevermore. For these substances cause the state no harm, they do but help citizens in their labor and leisure. One may purchase several grams of *coke* in any apothecary for the standard government price: two and a half rubles. Every apothecary is equipped with counters where a workingman may come in the morning or at his midday break and have a snort, in order to return, energized, to work for the good of the Russian state. They sell syringes with invigorating *angel dust*, and cigarettes with relaxing *weed*. True, *weed* is sold only after five o'clock. Now, if we're talking about *horse*, *acid*, and *mushrooms*, these substances really do poison the people. They weaken, flurry, and deprive them of will, and in so doing bring great harm to the government. For this very reason they are forbidden throughout the entire territory of Russia. This has all been wisely thought out. But these little fish—they are matchless, far above all your *coke-horses* taken together. They resemble a heavenly rainbow—they come, bring joy, and leave. After the sterlet rainbow there's no hangover or *withdrawal*.

The door opens with the blow of a metal-tipped boot. Only our Batya enters that way.

"Komiaga, you here already?"

"Where else would I be, Batya?"

I toss the sphere to Batya. He catches it, looks at it through the light, squinting.

"Ah . . . good!"

Shelet, Samosya, Yerokha, Mokry, and Pravda follow Batya in. Batya's entire *right* hand. In other places, with the *left*, Batya suppresses his *excitement*. That's as it should be—in such affairs it doesn't do to mix left with right.

Everyone's already a tad *edgy*. What do you expect? The fish are right at hand. Samosya's dark eyes flit back and forth and his fists are clenched. Yerokha's cheekbones bulge, he's clenching his teeth. Under drooping eyebrows, his teary walleye stares intently, as though he wants to bore a hole in me. Last time, he was the one who found the fish. Pravda always keeps his knife at hand—just a habit. His fist blanches as he squeezes it. All the right-side oprichniks are like that—fiery fellows. They'll fly off the handle, snuff 'em without flinching.

But Batya reins our guys in.

"Shoo!"

He places the sphere on the stone floor and is the first to take off his clothes. Servants aren't supposed to be here—we dress and undress ourselves. The oprichniks take off their brocaded jackets, peel off their silk shirts; we walk around naked and each of us takes his place on his lounge chair.

I lie down, covering my privates with my palms, and the shakes begin: *golden* ecstasy awaits just around the corner. As always, Batya does the *launching*. Baring himself, he takes the sphere with the fish and walks over . . . to me, of course. I was the procurer today. Therefore I'm the first of the seven. The first little fish is mine. I stretch my left arm out to Batya, squeezing and pumping my fist, pressing my forearm with the fingers of my right hand. Batya leans over my arm, like the Lord of the Hosts. He places the divine sphere on my swollen vein. I see the fish grow still, rocking in their aquarium. One of them is pulled in the direction of the vein pressed to the sphere. It wiggles its tiny little tail, drills through the supple glass, and pierces my vein. That's it! Hail to you! Tiny golden fish!

Batya moves over to Yerokha. He's already shaking, clenching his teeth, squeezing his fist, pumping his vein up stiff. Batya-Saboath the Bare-Assed leans over him . . .

But my eyes are not directed toward them. I see the vein in my left arm. I see it clearly. The teensy, millimeter-long tail of the golden sterlet peeps out from the pale bend of my elbow, straight out of the middle of my swollen vein.

O, divine instant when the golden fish enters the bloodstream! You are beyond compare, unlike any earthly pleasure, closest to what our forebear Adam experienced in the thickets of paradise, when he tasted of the invisible fruits created for him alone by the gray-bearded Saboath, Lord of the Hosts himself.

The little golden tail wiggles and the fish hides inside me. It swims along with the bloodstream. A trickle of blood shoots out in a fine fountain from a tiny hole. I press on my vein, throw my head back on the soft headrest, and close my eyes. I feel the golden sterlet swimming inside me, feel how it moves up along my vein, like it does in spring, striving to reach the spawning grounds at the headwaters of Mother Volga. Up, up, and farther upward! The golden sterlet has a destination to reach—my brain. My brain waits immobile in exalted anticipation: the sterlet-enchantress will deposit her heavenly caviar in my gray matter. Swim, oh swim, little fish of gold, rush unimpeded, spray your golden caviar into my tired brain, and may those roe-berries hatch into Worlds Grand, Sublime, Stupendous. May my brain rise from its slumber.

I count aloud with dry, chapped lips:
    One.
    Two.
    Three . . .

Ah, how my eyes they opened wide,
That's right, my eyes, yellow eyelet eyes,
Yellow eyelet eyes on my head, my crown,
On my crown, on my head so mighty.
And my crown—o this lovely head of mine,
Sits atop a neck that's long, it is, and strong,
Strong and long it is, and serpentine,
Clad in serpents' scales it is,
And sitting by this fabled head of mine,
Are six heads fine, and they do writhe, they do,
They twist and coil, and wink and blink
Their golden eyelet yellow eyes, they do.

They wink and bicker,
They spit and sputter,
Their jaws are red, so scarlet, so marvelous,

Gums of pink and teeth so sharp,
An acrid smoke pours from these jaws, it does,
This smoke rolls out and fire flares,
To bellowing and a mighty roar.

And for every head there is a name that's his,
A name that's sworn in brotherhood.
The first head is nicknamed Batya,
The next is called Komiaga,
The third is nicknamed Shelet,
The fourth goes by Samosya,
The fifth is called Yerokha,
The sixth is called Mokry,
The seventh is simply Pravda.
But all of us, seven-headed us,
I call Gorynych the Terrible—
The fire-breathing Dragon Ruinator.

And all seven heads sit on a torso,
A wide and broad, a stocky one.
On a stocky trunk, on a weighty one,
With a heavy tail, a sinuous one.
And that torso so exemplary
Is carried by legs, two thickset ones,
Both stout and thickset mighty ones,
With claws that stab the brittle earth, they do.

On the sides of the thickset trunk you see
Two webbed wings stretch and grow,
Webbed are they and sinewy,
Strong, and flapping forcefully.
They sweep the air most gloriously,
Tense and taut, they rise, they do.

Wrench away from our mother earth,
We rise right there, above our native land,
Above the earth, the whole Russian land,
And fly through the sky, the blue sky we do
Fly easily, wherever we want to go.

And the seventh head asks:
"Where are we flying, where does our path lead?"
And the sixth head asks:
"What lands are in our plans today?"
And the fifth head asks:
"Must we fly far, through the sky today?"
And the fourth head asks:
"Where should we turn our valiant wings today?"
And the third head asks:
"Which winds will wag our tails today?"
And the second head asks:
"What lands do we set our sights upon?"

Then the first head, the head of heads,
The greatest of all, replies to them:
"We'll fly right across the sky, we will,
Straight across the sky so blue,
Straight west to a land far away we will,
To a land far away, and wealthy, too,
A land beyond the crash of the ocean blue,
A far-flung land, yes, one that's flourishing,
Rich with gold and silver treasure nourishing.

In that far-off country towers stand,
Towers high and higher stand,
Tall, pointy and sharp they are,
Mercilessly buttressing the sky so blue,

And in the towers brazen people live,
Brazen and dishonest they live, they do,
They live with no fear of God they do,
These godless people,
They wallow in filthy sin, they do.
They wallow and enjoy themselves,
Mocking all that's sacred, all that's holy, too,
Mocking, jeering, and sneering is all they do,
They hide in Satan's work,
And spit on Sacred Rus, they do,
On the onion domes of Russia's Orthodox,
They all defame the golden name of God,
They flout the truth, oh yes, they do.

Now we fly most easily,
Through endless skies of baby blue,
Through nearby merchant countries,
Through groves and piney backwoods, too,
Through fields and meadows greening,
Through lakes and rivers clear as day,
Through villages and European towns,
Then we fly ferociously,
Far away from home, across the ocean-sea
Far away to where the godless roam.

We spread our webbed wings,
We wag our tail to the seven winds,
Our wings catch hold of the swift eighth wind,
The speedy eighth, the wind that travels the way we want to go,
We fly into its wake, stream into its wake, we do,
We saddle it, yes, straddle it, like a dashing stallion,
We ride the wild and galloping, we ride the rolling winds,
We take off on the winds, on a journey wild and dangerous.

We fly the first ten days,
We fly the first ten nights.
Ten days and nights over glassy water smooth,
Over the steep and rolling waves.
Our webbed wings weaken,
Our Gorynych heads grow weary,
Our mighty tail droops,
Our feet flail, our claws unclench.

Then, lo and behold on the ocean-sea,
We spy a metal house, on poles, on iron ones,
Built to pump and suck our mother earth,
To drink her deepest blood, amassed throughout the centuries,
We land atop that iron house,
We tear apart the iron roof,
We eat the twelve impious there,
And spit their bones into the sea.
We rest three days, and then three nights,
On the fourth we set the house afire,
And head off to the west again.

We fly ten days again,
And ten nights more,
Ten days, ten nights, the glassy waters o'er,
'Til our webbed wings weaken,
Our Gorynych heads droop,
Our mighty tail lolls, half dead
Our feet, our claws unclench.

Lo and behold in the ocean-sea we see
A mammoth six-decked ship.
A massive vessel floating east, it does,
From a wily country, from the godless land.

Bearing vile and filthy goods,
Carrying godless people,
Subversive letters and seditious documents,
Bearing delights demonical,
Bringing pleasures satanical,
Conveying decaying whore-swans
Like a whirlwind we attack that ship, we do,
Scorching and burning it from seven heads,
From seven heads and seven mouths,
We burn, we obliterate the godless filth within,
We gorge on decaying whore-swans, oh yes.
We rest three days, and rest three nights,
And on the fourth day we move on.

We fly another ten days,
And a third ten nights.
When lo we glimpse the godless land.
We fly, we fly, and fly anon.
We torch, we scorch it from seven heads,
From seven heads, from seven mouths,
We smite and bite the godless ones.

When we've had our fill of them, we spit out their bones, and
again we char the vermin, the vile parasites, those disgusting
whoresons, brazen and godless, who've forgotten everything sacred, everything thrice-sacred, they must be like the spawn of
Asmodeus like cockroaches like stinking rats scorched mercilessly to ashes we scorch whoresons the accursed burned to a
crisp, we do, with pure and honest fire, burn and burn and when
I slam against the hard glass window the first time it holds I slam
it the second time it cracks slam it the third time it breaks I stick
my head into the dark apartment the vermin hid from heavenly

judgment but my yellow eyes see in the dark they see well my yellow eyes and I stare and find the first foul creature a forty-two-year-old man wedged in a wardrobe I set the wardrobe on fire I watch the wardrobe burn he sits inside and doesn't budge he's scared and the wardrobe burns the wood crackles and he sits there and I wait he can't stand it and flings the door open with a cry and I send a thin stream of flame, my faithful skewer of flame into his mouth and he swallows my fire and falls I keep searching I find two children two little girls six and seven hiding under the bed under the wide bed I drench the bed in a wide stream the bed burns the pillows flame the blanket they can't stand it they scramble out from under the bed run to the door I send a fan of fire after them they run as far as the door burning both of them I keep on searching I'm searching for the sweetest thing of all and I find her a woman thirty years old blond who hides frightened in the bath between the washing machine and the wall dressed only in her nightgown her knees are bare she's squatting petrified she looks at me with fear, her eyes wide and round, and slowly my nostrils inhale her sleepy smell I move closer to her closer closer closer I look and tenderly I touch her knees with my nose and slowly spread spread spread her and send my thinnest stream my faithful flaming skewer into her narrow womb I send it and its might fills her trembling womb, my flaming skewer fills it she howls inhuman cries and slowly my fiery flaming skewer begins to fuck her to fuck her to **fuck fuckfuckfuckfuckfuckfuckfuckfuckfuck**.

Awakening . . .

It's like rising from the dead. Returning to your old body, which died long ago and is buried in the ground. Oh, how loath you are to do so!

I lift my leaden eyelids and see my naked self stretched out on the lounge chair. I stir, cough, sit up. I'm hot. I grab a bottle of icy Esenin birch juice. Koliakha said he'd provide the birch juice, and he didn't forget. It gurgles in my parched throat. The others are also stirring, coughing. How good. It's always good on fish. Never been any *nasty crash* or *black slough* on fish. This isn't any of your miserable smack.

italics = intensifies

We all cough as we wake up. Batya gulps his juice down. His pale face is sweating. Drinking your fill is the first order of business after fish. The second is belching. And the third is telling who did what.

We drink and belch.

We share what we've been through. This is the eighth time we've been the many-headed dragon Gorynych. Fish are a collective affair; only an idiot uses them alone.

As usual, Batya's not very pleased.

"Why're you always in such a hurry? You're always wanting to burn or eat . . . You're all fretting and fidgeting—first this way, then that. Calm down, fellows, one thing at a time."

"It's all because Shelet's itching to start," Yerokha says, coughing. "You're always rushing to be on time, brother."

"Oh, come on now," says Shelet, stretching. "It was good, wasn't it? I liked the part with the ship . . . the way they crawled through the portholes and jumped into the water!"

Mokry nods. "Great! But I liked that part in the city best: how we made a fan with seven streams, and the way they squealed in the skyscraper . . . cool! And Komiaga over there, isn't he a genius? The way he did her! Smoke was comin' out of that American broad's asshole!"

"Komiaga's inventive! He studied at the university, fuckin' A!" Pravda grins.

Batya gives it to him on the lips—for cursing.

"Sorry, Batya, the devil led me astray." Pravda makes a face.

"All in all—it was good," Batya sums up. "They were the *right kind* of fish!"

"*The right kind!*" We all agree.

We dress.

If the gold sterlets are good you don't feel weak afterward, just the opposite: you're stronger. Like you've been at a resort in our sunny Crimea. Like it's the end of September outside, and you just spent three weeks in Koktebel lying on the golden sand and submitting various limbs to sinuous Tatar massage. And now you've returned to Whitestone Moscow, landed at Vnukovo, disembarked from the silvery airplane, taken a deep breath of the Moscow country air, held it in—and right away you feel so good, your soul feels so *perfect*, so balanced, so *important* . . . you realize that life is good, you are strong, you're part of a great endeavor, and your confederates are waiting for you, a daring bold fellow who's up to his ears in urgent work. The enemy hasn't lessened in number, His Majesty is alive and well, and, most important of all: Russia is alive and well, rich, huge, united. Over the course of those three weeks our Mother Russia hasn't budged; quite the contrary, her eternal roots have delved even deeper into the earth's meat.

Batya is right: after fish you feel like living and working, but after *horse* you only want to run and find another dose.

I glance at the clock—I spent only forty-three minutes Gorynyching, but inside it feels like an entire life. And this life gives me new strength to fight our adversaries and root out subversion. I have quite a few questions about the fish: if they are so helpful to us, the oprichniks, why not make them legal, at least for us *exclusively*? Batya has conveyed our thoughts on this score to His Majesty more than once, but the response is adamant: the law is the same for all.

We come out of the bathhouse energized and seemingly more youthful. Each of us gives a half-ruble to tattooed Koliakha. He bows, pleased.

It's frosty outside, but the sun has already hidden itself, rolled behind the clouds. Time to return to business. Right now, I've got a *star-fall* on my hands. It's necessary business, state business.

I get in my Mercedov, drive onto Shabolovka Street, and call in: Is everything ready? It seems everything is.

I reach for my cigarettes—after fish I always feel like smoking. But I'm out. I brake near a People's Kiosk. The merchant is all red in the face, like Petrushka in the street shows. He leans out:

"What does your honor desire, Sir Oprichnik?"

"I desire cigarettes."

"We have filtered and unfiltered Rodina."

"Filtered. Three packs."

"At your service. Smoke to your health."

It seems the fellow has a sense of humor. Taking out my wallet, I look at the kiosk window. It's the standard selection: Rodina cigarettes and "Russia" cardboard-filtered *papirosy*, "rye" and wheat vodka, white and black bread, two types of chocolates—Mishka the Bear and Mishka in the North—apple and plum jam, butter and vegetable oil, meat with and without bones, whole and baked milk, chicken eggs and quail eggs, boiled and smoked sausage, cherry and pear drink, and finally—"Russian" cheese.

His Majesty's father, the late Nikolai Platonovich, had a good idea: liquidate all the foreign supermarkets and replace them with Russian kiosks. And put two types of each thing in every kiosk, so the people have a choice. A wise decision, profound. Because our God-bearing people should choose from two things, not from three or thirty-three. Choosing one of two creates spiritual calm, people are imbued with certainty in the future, superfluous fuss and bother is avoided, and consequently—*everyone is satisfied*. And when a people such as ours is *satisfied*, great deeds may be accomplished.

Everything about the kiosks is fine; there's only one thing I can't wrap my head around. Why is it that all the goods are in pairs, like the beasts on Noah's Ark, but there's only one kind of cheese, Russian? My logic is helpless here. Well, this sort of thing isn't for us to decide, but for His Majesty. From the Kremlin His Majesty sees the people better, they're more visible. All of us down below crawl about like lice, hustling and bustling; we don't recognize the true path. But His Majesty sees everything, hears everything. He knows who needs what.

I light up.

A vendor approaches me. He's got a neat beard, wears a neat caftan, and has good manners. The tray he carries, strapped over his shoulders, is for books—that's obvious.

"Would his honor Mr. Oprichnik, sir, care to acquire the most recent novelties of Russian literature?"

He unfolds his three-part tray in front of me. Bookstands are also standardized, approved by His Majesty and approved by the Literary Chamber. Our people respect books. On the left side there's Orthodox Church literature; on the right the Russian classics; and in the middle, the latest works by contemporary writers. First I look over the prose of our country's contemporary writers: Ivan Korobov's *White Birch*; Nikolai Voropaevsky's *Our Fathers*; Isaak Epshtein's *The Taming of the Tundra*; Rashid Zametdinov's *Russia—My Motherland*; Pavel Olegov's *The Nizhny Novgorod Tithe*; Savvaty Sharkunov's *Daily Life of the Western Wall*; Irodiada Deniuzhkina's *My Heart's Friend*; Oksana Podrobskaya's *The Mores of New Chinese Children*. I know all these authors well. They're famous, distinguished. Caressed by the love of the people and His Majesty.

"Let's see . . . what's this here?" In the corner of the tray I notice a textbook by Mikhail Shveller on developing carpenters for parish schools.

And under it—a textbook on carpentry by the same author.

"There are two schools not far from here, Sir Oprichnik. The parents buy them."

"I see. Any young prose?"

"We're expecting new works by young authors in the spring, as always, for the Easter Book Fair."

Got it.

My eyes move to Russian poetry: Pafnuty Sibirsky, "The Motherland's Expanses"; Ivan Manot-Bely, "The Color of Apple Trees"; Antonina Ivanova, "Russia's Loyal Sons"; Pyotr Ivanov's "Water Meadow"; Isai Bershtein's "I Have You to Thank for Everything!"; Ivan Petrosky's "Live, Life!"; Salman Basaev's "Song of the Chechen Mountains"; Vladislav Syrkov's "His Majesty's Childhood."

I pick up the last book and open it. It's a long poem about His Majesty's childhood. The poet Syrkov already wrote about

His youth and adulthood a long time ago. An elegant publication: expensive calfskin binding, gold lettering, pink page edges, thick white paper, and a bookmark of blue silk. On the half-title there's a lively portrait of the poet: a bit gloomy, gray-haired, stooped. He's at the seashore, gazing out toward the horizon; the ocean waves crash and crash, crash and crash against the rock where he stands. He somehow resembles an eagle owl, and seems deeply immersed in himself.

"An extraordinary, spiritually uplifting poem, Sir Oprichnik," says the peddler in a businesslike voice. "Such a vivid portrait of His Majesty, such lively language . . ."

I read:

How you ran, so alive and so cheerful,
How you played in the river and sand,
How you traveled to school, never tearful,
How you whispered, "my dear, native land,"

How you strove to be honest and steady,
How you learned about freedom from birds,
How your answers were swift, always ready,
How you tugged on the braids of the girls,

How athletic you grew, and how stubborn,
How you wanted to know all apace,
How you loved your sweet good-hearted mother,
How your father you walked to the gates,

How you ran with the dogs 'cross the valleys
How you studied the crops and the sod,
How in winter's grim blizzards you rallied,
How by spring you maneuvered the yacht,

How you learned to fly huge helicopters,
How you crafted your own paper kite,
How you galloped on fleet-footed Topper,
How whole poems in Chinese you'd recite,

How you penned your calligraphy ably,
How at dawn you would shoot at the range,
How you copied the character "guo jia,"*
How with Father you flew a small plane,

How your Motherland swiftly awakened,
How dear Russia in you did resound,
How by Nature your spirit was shapen,
How abruptly your own time came 'round.

Well, not bad. A bit overly emotional, as always with Syrkov, but on the other hand—quite vivid. The peddler is right. I'll buy the book, read it, and then give it to Posokha, so he reads this poem instead of that obscene *Secret Tales*.

"How much?" I ask.

"For everyone else, three rubles, but for Sir Oprichnik, two and a half."

Not cheap. But then it would be a sin to scrimp on His Majesty's life story. I hand over the money. The peddler accepts it with a bow. Sticking the book in my pocket, I get into the Mercedov.

And step on the gas.

* State (*Chin.*).

P*utting out* stars is harder than mixing honey and water," our Batya likes to say. And it's true. Nonetheless, it's an important affair, an affair of state. But skill is needed, a special approach. In a word, it's an "intelligent" affair. And intelligent hands are needed. You have to invent or fabricate something every time. It's nothing like burning down Zemsky mansions.

Therefore, I head back for the center of town again. I drive along crowded Yakimanka, again in the red lane. I drive onto the Great Stone Bridge. The sun has peeked out from behind the winter clouds, illuminating the Kremlin. And it is shining. How marvelous that for the last twelve years its walls have been painted white. And instead of those demonic pentacles on the Kremlin towers the state's two-headed eagles shine gold.

The Kremlin is glorious in clear weather! It glows. The Palace of the Russian Government blinds the eyes, it takes your breath away. The Kremlin walls and towers sparkle like white lumps of sugar, the cupolas reflect the sun tinsel gold, the Ladder of Paradise bell tower of Ioann Lestvichnik rises in the air like an arrow. Blue-tinted firs surround it like stern guards, and Russia's flag flies proud and free. Here, just over the crenellated, blindingly white, stone walls, is the heart of the Russian land, the throne of our state, the core and hub of Mother Russia. There's nothing shameful in laying down your life for the sugary white Kremlin and its towers, the majestic eagles, the flag, the relics of Russia's rulers reposing in the Cathedral of the Archangel, Riurik's sword, the crown of Monomakh, the Tsar-Pushka cannon, the Tsar-Kolokol bell tower, the pavestones of Red Square, for Uspensky Cathedral or the Kremlin towers. And there's no shame in laying down a second life—for His Majesty.

Tears well up in my eyes . . .

I turn on to Vozdvizhenka Street. My mobilov pesters me with three cracks of the whip: it's the captain of the Good Fellows, reporting that they've got everything ready for the *extinguishing*. But he wants to clarify details, elucidate, sort out, brainstorm, go over things. He's not sure of himself, that's obvious. *That's why I'm coming to see you, you dimwit!* Young Count Ukhov from the Inner Circle runs this show, and the order answers directly to His Majesty. Their full name is the Fellowship of Russian Good Fellows for Good. They're young blades, zealous, upright, but they need supervision, because their leadership went awry from the very beginning—no luck with brainy types, no matter what you do! Each year His Majesty changes their captain, but not much changes. It's baffling . . . In the Oprichnina we nicknamed these ruffians "Good-for-Noughts." Not all they do turns out for the good, oh no, not by a long shot . . . But that's all right, we'll help. We'll lend a hand, not for the first time.

I drive up to their richly decorated headquarters. They don't have much in the way of brains, but they've got money coming out of their asses. Suddenly—there's a red call on my mobilov. Something important. It's Batya:

"Komiaga, where are you?"

"Heading for the Good-for-Noughts, Batya."

"The devil take them. I want you off to Orenburg—fast. Our guys have locked horns with customs."

"That's the left *wing*'s problem, Batya, I'm a *former* in that business."

"Chapyzh is burying his mother, Seryi and Vosk are in a meeting with Count Savelev in the Kremlin, and Samosya, the idiot, ran into one of the Streltsy on Ostozhenka Street."

So that's it.

"What about Baldokhai?"

"On a business trip, in Amsterdam. Come on, Komiaga, get over there while they still haven't bamboozled us. You worked in customs, you know the ins and outs. It's a serious *haul*, around a hundred thousand. If it falls through, we'll never forgive ourselves. As it is, those customs guys have gotten too cheeky lately. Go sort it out!"

"Work and Word!, Batya."

Hmm. Orenburg. That means—the Road. There's no joking with the Road. It's worth drawing blood for it. I call the Good-for-Noughts and reschedule for the evening:

"I'll be there by the time the wailing starts!"

I turn on to the boulevard, then over the Great Stone Bridge again and into the Kaluzhskaya-2 Underground Highway. It's a good road, wide and smooth. I accelerate to 260 versts per hour, and eighteen minutes later I'm at Vnukovo Airport. I park my Mercedov in the government parking lot and enter the terminal. A young woman steps forward to greet me in the blue uniform of Aeroflot: with aiguillettes, silver embroidery, Hessian boots, and white leather gloves. She invites me into the security corridor. I place my right hand against the glass square. My whole life appears in the pine-scented air: date of birth, rank, home address, status, chart of habits, physical-mental characteristics, birthmarks, illnesses, psychosomatics, my character core, preferences, prejudices, size of my limbs and organs. The girl gazes at my mind and body, distinguishing, comparing. "Full and complete transparency," as His Majesty says. And thank God: we're in our own homeland, nothing to be shy about.

"What is your desired destination, Mr. Oprichnik, sir?" she asks.

"Orenburg," I answer. "First class."

"Your airplane departs in twenty-one minutes. The cost of the ticket is twelve rubles. Duration of the flight is fifty minutes. How would you prefer to pay?"

"In cash."

Nowadays we always pay for everything with genuine coins.

"With which kind?"

"The second mintage."

"Wonderful." She fills in the ticket, stirring the air with her sparkling gloves.

I hand over the money: a gold ten-ruble piece with His Majesty's noble profile, and two rubles. They disappear into the frosted glass wall.

"This way, please," she says, directing me toward the first-class waiting room with a half-bow.

I enter. A man in a white *papakha* hat and a white Cossack uniform takes my outer clothes with a low bow. I hand him the black caftan and hat. In the spacious first-class lounge there aren't many travelers: two richly dressed Cossack families, four quiet Europeans, an old Chinese man with a small boy, a noble with three servants, some woman traveling alone, and two loud, tipsy merchants. And all of them, with the exception of the woman and the Chinese, are eating something. The tavern is good. I know, I've eaten here a number of times. And after golden sterlets you always feel like having a bite. I sit down at a table and immediately a *trans-*

parent waiter appears, as though he'd come right out of Gogol's immortal pages—plump cheeks, red lips, crimped hair, a smile:

"What, may I inquire, is your desire, sir?"

"My desire, friend, is drink, appetizers, and a light meal."

"We have rye vodka with gold or silver sand, Shanghai sturgeon caviar, Taiwanese smoked fillet of sturgeon, marinated milk mushrooms in sour cream, jellied beef aspic, Moscow perch in aspic, Guangdong ham."

"Give me the silver rye, mushrooms in sour cream, and the jellied beef. And what do you have to eat?"

"A nice sterlet soup, Moscow borsht, duck with turnip, rabbit in noodles, charcoal-grilled trout, grilled beef with potatoes."

"The fish soup. And a glass of sweet kvass."

"Thank you kindly."

The *transparent* disappears. You could talk about anything at all with him, even about Saturn's moons. His memory is basically boundless. Once, when I was in my cups, I asked the local *transparent* the formula for viviparous fibers. He told me. And went on to describe the technical production process in great detail. Our Batya, when he's had a bit to drink, has one question he likes to ask the *transparent*: "How much time remains until the sun explodes?" They answer precisely within a year . . . But now—there's no time for boldness, and besides, I'm hungry.

The order immediately arises from the table. That's the kind of *handy* tables they have here. They always give you a carafe of vodka. I drink a shot, take a bite of marinated mushrooms in sour cream. Humankind has yet to invent any better *zakuska*. Even Nanny's half-sour pickles can't hold a candle to this. I consume an excellent piece of jellied beef aspic with mustard, drink the glass of sweet kvass in one gulp, and set to work on the fish soup. You must always eat it slowly. I look around. The merchants are polishing off their second carafe, jabbering on about some "third-level magnetic tape sorter" and 100-horsepower paracletes they bought in Moscow. The Europeans talk quietly in English. The Cossacks mumble in their own language, wolfing pastries and washing them down with tea. The Chinese man and boy chew on something of their own from a bag. The lady smokes aloofly. Finishing the soup, I order a cup of Turkish coffee, pull out my cigarettes, and light up. I put in a call to our guys on the Road: I need to get up to speed. Potrokha's face appears. I switch the mobilov to secret conversation mode. Potrokha rattles off the main points:

"Twelve trailers; 'High Fashion'; 'Shanghai-Tirana.' We put a little fly in their ointment, stopped them right after the gates, drove them straightaway onto the sample clarifier, but the insurance guys dug in their heels—they were paid by the old docket, they don't want to cook up a new contract. We lean on them through the chamber, but the head honcho says they have their own interests with those merchants, there's a *wet* petition; we go back to customs, but they're getting a piece of the action, too, the chief closes the case, and the clerk *turns*. The upshot—they'll let them go in two hours."

"Got it." I start thinking.

In these kinds of affairs you need to be a good chess player, to think ahead. This case isn't simple, but it's clear. Since the Customs Department clerk *turned*, they must have a *corridor with clout*, and they renewed the contract right after the frontier post. So that means they went through the Kazakhs *clean*. It's obvious: customs closed down so they could *smile* at the western gates. They'll hand in the second contract, pay in white, then they'll tear up the insurance contract, and the Western clerks will draw up a four-hour report. Then they'll hide the mole, sign a clean contract—and twelve trailers of "High Fashion" will sail off to the Albanian city of Tirana. And customs will get the better of us again.

I think. Potrokha waits.

"Here you go, man. Take the *cardiac*, made a deal with the clerk about a *white* discussion, take the *greased* junior clerk to the meeting, and get your physicians in place. Do you guys have a *rotten* contract with you?"

"Of course. What time should I set the meeting?"

I look at my watch:

"In an hour and a half."

"You got it."

"And tell the clerk that I *have it*."

"Understood."

I put away the mobilov. I put out my cigarette. The plane is already boarding. I place my palm on the table, thank the *transparent* for the meal, and walk down a delicate pink hallway that smells like blossoming acacia into the airplane. It's not big, but it's comfortable—a Boeing-Itsendi 797. Not surprisingly, there are signs in Chinese everywhere. He who builds the Boeings orders the music. I enter the first-class cabin and sit down. Other than me there are three people in first class—the old Chinese man with the boy, and that lone woman. All three of the Russian newspapers are available: *Rus*, *Kommersant*, and *Vozrozhdenie*. I already know all the news and don't feel like reading about it *on paper*.

The plane takes off.

I ask for tea, and order an old movie: *Striped Passage*. On business trips I always watch old comedies; just a habit. This one's a good little flick, cheery, even though it's Soviet. You watch lions and tigers being transported on a ship; they break out of their cages and scare people. And you start thinking—those were Russian people living back then, during the Red Troubles. And they really weren't all that different from us. Except that almost all of them were atheists.

I take a look to see what the others are watching: the

Chinese—*River Factories*, that makes sense; but the lady . . .
oh-ho, now that's interesting—*The Great Russian Wall*. I would
never have said by her looks that she'd like that sort of film. *The
Great Russian Wall* . . . It was made about ten years ago by our
great director Fyodor Baldev, nicknamed "Fyodor-the-Bare-
Who-Ate-the-Bear." The most important movie in the history of
Russia's Revival. The film is about the plot hatched by the Ambassadorial Department and the Duma, the construction of the
Western Wall, and His Majesty's battle; about the first oprichniks, heroic Valuya and Zveroga, who perished at the dacha of
the traitorous minister. The whole affair went down in Russian
history as the plan to "Saw and Sell." What a hullabaloo that
film caused, how many arguments, how many questions and answers! How many cars and faces were bashed in because of it!
The actor who played His Majesty entered a monastery afterward. I haven't watched it for a very, very long time. But I remember it by heart. For the oprichniks it's a kind of textbook.

I can see the face of the minister of foreign affairs on the blue
bubble, and his accomplice, the chairman of the Duma. They're
composing the terrible agreement on the division of Russia at the
minister's dacha.

CHAIRMAN OF THE DUMA: So, we take power. But what do we
do with Russia, Sergei Ivanovich?
MINISTER: Saw it up and sell it.
CHAIRMAN: To whom?
MINISTER: We sell the east to the Japanese; Siberia goes to the
Chinese; the Krasnodarsk region—to the Ukies; Altai—to
the Kazakhs; Pskov Oblast—to the Estonians; Novgorod
Oblast—to the Belorussians. But we'll leave the center for
ourselves. Everything is ready, Boris Petrovich. We've not
only handpicked all our people, they're already in place.

(A significant pause. A candle burns.)

Tomorrow! What do you say?

CHAIRMAN *(looking around)*: It's a bit scary, Sergei Ivanovich . . .

MINISTER *(breathing hot and heavy, embracing the Duma chairman)*: Don't be afraid, don't be scared! Together we'll control Moscow! Eh? Moscow?

(He squints lustfully.)

Think about it, my dear fellow! We'll have all of Moscow right here!

(He shows his pudgy palm.)

Come now, will you sign?

Then there's a close-up: the eyes of the Duma chairman. First they look back and forth, intimidated, frightened, like a wolf brought to bay. Then anger awakens in them, intensifying to a furious rage. Menacing music grows louder, a disturbing, slanted shadow falls, the night wind billows the curtains and blows out the candle; a dog begins to bark. In the dark the chairman clenches his fists, at first shaking with fear, then with anger and hatred for the Russian state.

CHAIRMAN *(clenching his teeth)*: I'll sign it all!

He's a good director, Fedya Baldev. It was no accident that right after this film came out His Majesty appointed him head of the Cinema Chamber. But this lady . . . she looks like a noble. And for the nobility this film is like a stab in the heart. The lady looks at the film on the bubble as though she weren't seeing anything. Her face is cold, indifferent. It's not very pretty, but clearly pedigreed. You can tell she didn't grow up in some Novoslobodsk orphanage.

I can't help myself:

"Excuse me, madame, do you like that film?"

She turns her well-groomed face toward me:

"Quite, Mr. Oprichnik."

Not a muscle in her face twitches. Totally calm, like a snake.

"Is this an official inquiry?"

"Not at all. It's just that there's a great deal of blood in this film."

"You think that Russian women are afraid of blood?"

"All women are afraid of blood. And Russian . . ."

"Mr. Oprichnik, thanks to you and your colleagues, Russian women have long since grown accustomed to blood. To amounts small and large."

Whoa! Can't catch her bare-handed!

"Perhaps, but . . . It seems to me that there are far more pleasant films for the female eye. And this one contains a lot of suffering."

"Everyone has their preferences, Mr. Oprichnik. You recall the love song 'It Matters Not Whether I Love or Suffer' . . ."

Somehow she's way too haughty.

"Forgive me, I was just asking."

"And I am just answering." She turns away and again stares coldly at the screen.

She intrigues me. I take her picture on my mobilov, and give the signal for our security service to *pinhole* this lady. The answer comes immediately: Anastasia Petrovna Stein-Sotskaya, daughter of the Duma clerk Sotsky. Holy Mother of God! The very same clerk who worked on the pernicious plan to "Saw and Sell" with the Duma chairman. I wasn't yet in the oprichnina during those strife-filled years. I was working quietly in customs with antiques and precious metals . . . I understand, yes, I understand why she's looking at the film *that way*. Why, it's her family history, for heaven's sake! If memory serves, Sotsky was beheaded on Red Square shortly thereafter, along with nine other plotters . . .

On my bubble there are tigers in cages and Soviet cooks, but I look right through them. Right here, next to me, is a victim of the Russian state. What did they do with her? She didn't even change her surname, she took a hyphenated one. Proud. I order a detailed biography: thirty-two years old, married to the textile merchant Boris Stein, spent six years in exile with her mother and younger brother, got a law degree, character core "Running Sister—18," left-handed, broken collar bone, weak lungs, bad teeth, miscarried two times, the third gave birth to a boy, lives in Orenburg, enjoys archery, chess, playing guitar, and singing Russian love songs.

I turn off my tigers and try to doze.

But thoughts keep welling up: here's this person sitting close by who holds a grudge for all time. Not only against us oprichniks, but against His Majesty. And nothing can be done about it. But she's raising a son, and she and Stein probably have open house on Thursdays; the Orenburg intelligentsia probably gathers. They sing old songs, drink tea with cherry preserves, and then they have—*conversations*. And you don't have to be the clairvoyant Praskovia to guess what and *who* they are talking about . . .

And *after everything* that's happened, there are hundreds upon hundreds of these people. If you count their children, husbands, and wives—thousands upon thousands. Now that's a substantial force, which needs to be taken into *account*. Now you need to think ahead, calculate your plays. And the fact that they've been kicked out of their well-feathered Moscow nests and stuffed into Orenburgs and Krasnoyarsks doesn't help, it's not a *solution*. In a word: His Majesty is merciful. And thank God . . .

I manage to drift off after all.

Even in my sleep I see something fleeting and slipping away. But not a white stallion—something small, crumbly, dreary . . .

I awake when they announce the landing. Out of the corner of my eye I glance at the bubble with the historical film: it's the denouement, the interrogation in the Secret Department, the rack, red-hot pokers, and the face of the minister, distorted by anger:

"I hate . . . how I hate you!"

And the finale, the last scenes: His Majesty, still young, stands against a familiar landscape, bathed in the light of the rising sun, holding the *first* brick in his hands; he looks toward the west and utters those familiar, beloved words:

"The Great Russian Wall!"

We land.

Potrokha meets me at the airplane: he's young, red-cheeked, snub-nosed, and has an overly gilded forelock. I get into his Mercedov and, as always, have the feeling that it's my car. Déjà vu. All oprichniks have identical cars, whether in Moscow, Orenburg, or Oimyakon: 400-horsepower Mercedov coupes the color of ripe tomatoes.

"Hi there, Potrokha."

"Hi, Komiaga."

We always call each other by the familiar form, *ty*, since we're one oprichnik family. Even though I'm about one and a half times older than Potrokha.

"Why aren't you catching any mice here? As soon as Chapyzh leaves, you all stop dead in your tracks."

"Don't get all steamed up, Komiaga. This affair's a matter of *grease*. They have a *hook* in the Department. Up till now, Chapyzh has been in *good* with them. I'm a nobody as far as they're concerned. A *shoulder* is what's needed."

"You need a left *shoulder* but I'm from the right!"

"It doesn't matter at this point, Komiaga. The main thing is—you have an Official Seal. When you've got a *disputed deal*, you need an oprichnik with authority."

I know, we've been through that. An oprichnik with authority. And that means the Official Seal. Only twelve oprichniks have the seal. It's in the left hand, in the palm, under the skin. And it can only be taken from me along with my hand.

"Did you set up a meeting with the clerk?"

"Of course. The *white* discussion is in a quarter of an hour."

"The physicians?"

"All there."

"Let's go!"

Potrokha drives deftly through the airport gates onto the highway, and steps on the gas. We race not to Orenburg—famous for its fine, intricate shawls and its narrow-eyed Russian-Chinese beauties—but in the opposite direction. Along the way Potrokha explains the situation to me in greater detail. It's been a long time since I worked with customs, a long time. Many *new* things have appeared in the meantime. Much that we couldn't have dreamed about back then. *Transparent* illegals have cropped up, for instance. There's this unexplained "export of empty spaces." Subtropical air is in demand in Siberia these days—they run air in *volumes.* From some kind of celestial devices with *compressed desires.* Go figure! Thank God today's business is simpler.

In a quarter of an hour Potrokha reaches the Road. It must be three years since I've been here. And each time I see it—it takes my breath away. The Road! It's an amazing thing. It runs from Guangzhou across China, then winds its way across Kazakhstan, enters through the gates in our Southern Wall, and then traverses the breadth of Mother Russia to Brest. From there—straight to Paris. The Guangzhou–Paris Road. Since the manufacturing of all necessary goods flowed over to Great China bit by bit, they built this Road to connect China to Europe. It's got ten lanes, and four tracks underground for high-speed trains. Heavy trailers crawl along the road with their goods 24/7, and the silvery trains whistle. It's a real feast for the eyes.

We drive closer.

The Road is surrounded by three layers of security, protecting it from saboteurs and lamebrained cyberpunks. We drive into a roadside stop. It's gorgeous, large, glass, built specially for long-distance drivers. You've got a winter garden with palms, a bathhouse with a pool, Chinese cookshops, Russian taverns, workout gyms, a hotel, a movie theater, a bordello with skilled whores, and even ice-skating rinks.

But Potrokha and I head for the meeting site. Everyone's sitting and waiting: the clerk from the Customs Department, the junior clerk from the same place, who's been *greased* by us, two guys from the Insurance Chamber, the commander of the Highway Department, and two Chinese representatives. Potrokha and I sit down and begin the discussion. A Chinese *xiao jie*, tea girl, comes in, brews white tea, a real tonic for the body, and pours some for everyone with a smile. The customs clerk digs in his heels and refuses to budge.

"The train is clean, the Kazakhs have no objections, the contract is point-to-point, everything's in order."

It's obvious that the whole train has *greased* the clerk, all twelve trailers, and all the way to Brest. Our goal is to detain the Chinese long enough that their highway insurance runs out, and then *our* insurance will kick in. And our insurance is 3 percent. Every last dog on the Road knows it. On this 3 percent the oprichnina treasury stays *quite* plump. And not only the oprichnina's. There's enough for all upright people; they'll all get something. This 3 percent covers a lot of legitimate expenses. And our expenses, as servants of His Majesty, are countless. Does the customs clerk, stuffed with yuan, really care?

The highway commander is *ours*. He starts *pumping*:

"Two of the trailers have counterfeit Chinese inspection stickers. We need an expert report."

The Chinese break in:

"The inspection is in order, here are the findings."

Shining characters of confirmation appear in the air. I learned conversational Chinese, of course; who could get along without it now? But the characters are just one big swamp for me. Potrokha, on the other hand, is nimble with Chinese; he dug up the findings on replacing the second turbine, and he illuminates it with a little thumbelinochka.

"Where's the quality certificate? The manufacturer's address? The lot number?"

"Shantou, Red Wealth factory, 380-6754069."

Hmm . . . The turbine's "local." The inspection sticker won't do it. Work on the Road is complicated now. Before, the trailers would simply be wrecked: the tires slashed, or windows all bashed in, or you'd slip something into the driver's noodles while he was eating. Nowadays they're on the lookout for these things. Yes, well, no matter. We have our own ways, tried and true. The tea is served by a *greased xiao jie.*

"Gentlemen, I consider this discussion to be concluded," says the clerk, and then he clutches his chest.

There's a big fuss and bustle: What happened?

"A heart attack!"

Now, how do you like that? And the *xiao jie* doesn't even blush. She bows and carries her tea tray out with her. The physicians appear and take the clerk away. He's moaning, and pale. We reassure him:

"You'll get better, Savely Tikhonovich!"

Of course he'll get better. The Chinese stand up—business is done. Not so quick. Now it's our turn: the last statement is directed to the *greased* junior clerk:

"Look here, the travel documents appear to have been backdated."

"What are you talking about? It's not possible! Let me see,

let me see . . ." The junior clerk stares walleyed at the travel documents, aims the thumbelinochka at them. "You're right! The blue imprint is smudged! Oh dear, highway robbers! They deceived our trusting Savely Tikhonovich! They took him in! Crooks! *Zui xing!*" This is a new turn of events. One of the Chinese mutters:

"No way! The travel document was notarized by both border committees."

"If a representative of the Russian customs has noticed a discrepancy, bilateral expertise is required," I answer. "In this dispute I represent our side, as an oprichnik with authority."

The Chinese are in a panic: gobs of time will be lost on this and their Chinese insurance will expire. And drawing up new travel permits, well, it's not like throwing together a fish-bone pie. You've got to get a health inspection, technical inspection, and border check done all over again, not to mention getting a visa from the Antimonopoly Chamber. So it all boils down to:

"Take out insurance, gentlemen."

The Chinese are wailing. Threats. Who, just who are you threatening, *sha bi*[†]? Complain to whomever you like. The commander of the Highway Department *sniffs* at the Chinese:

"Russian insurance is the best defense against cyberpunks."

The Chinese grit their teeth:

"Where's the seal?"

So why the hell did I fly here, you wonder? Here's the seal: I place my left palm on the square of frosted glass, leaving an Official Seal on it. And no more questions. Potrokha and I wink at each other: the 3 percent is ours! The Chinese walk out, all bent out of shape. The junior clerk leaves; he's done his *greasy* work. Only Potrokha and I remain.

---

* Crime! (*Chin.*).
† Asshole (*Chin.*).

"Thanks, Komiaga." Potrokha squeezes my wrist.

"Work and Word!, Potrokha."

We finish the tea and walk outside. It's colder here than in Moscow. We oprichniks have an *old* feud with customs, and there's no end in sight. It's all because customs is run by His Majesty's brother Alexander Nikolaevich, and will be run by him for a long time to come. And dear Alexander Nikolaevich can't stomach our Batya. Something happened between them, something that even His Majesty cannot reconcile. And nothing can be done about it—there was, is, and will be a war . . .

"We should rest a bit." Potrokha scratches his overgilded forelock and pushes his sable hat back on the nape of his neck. "Let's go to the bathhouse. They've got a good masseur. And there are two *hunanochki*.*"

He takes out his mobilov and shows me. Two charming Chinese girls appear in the air: one is riding naked on a buffalo, the other stands naked under a flowing waterfall.

"So?" Potrokha winks at me. "You won't regret it. Better than your Moscow girls. Eternal virgins."

I look at my watch: 15:00.

"No, Potrokha. I have to fly to Tobol next and then back to Moscow to snuff a *star*."

"As you like. Then to the airport?"

"That's right."

While he's driving, I look up the schedule of flights, and choose one. There's a one-hour break before the next flight, but I put the outgoing airplane on hold: they can friggin' wait. Potrokha and I say goodbye, I board the Orenburg–Tobol plane, and get in touch with Praskovia's security service, letting them know to meet me. I put on earphones, order Rimsky-Korsakov's *Scheherazade*. And fall asleep.

---

* Hunanese girl.

The stewardess wakes me with a gentle touch:

"Mr. Oprichnik, sir! We've already landed."

Marvelous. Taking a swig of Altai springwater, I disembark, and step onto a moving sidewalk that takes me into the huge terminal of the Yermak Timofeevich Airport. It's new, just built by the Chinese. I've already been here three times. And all on the same business—to see the clairvoyant.

Near the enormous figure of Yermak with his glowing sword, two goons from the great soothsayer's security service are waiting for me. Each of them is a head taller than me, and two times as wide, but nonetheless, next to Yermak's giant boot they look like field mice in red caftans.

I walk over to them. They bow and lead me to the car. As we leave the airport I manage to take a breath of the Tobol air: it's even colder here than in Orenburg. It's a good 32 below. Now here's that global warming foreigners are always blathering about. We still have snow and freezing weather in Russia, gentlemen, have no doubts.

They lead me to a powerful Chinese off-road vehicle, the Zhu-Ba-Ze, with a bumper that resembles a boar's snout. Nowadays these off-roaders are used all over Siberia. They're reliable, trouble-free in brutal winter conditions as well as in the heat. Siberians call them "Boars."

We first drive along the highway, then turn onto a narrow road. The captain from Moscow reports: everything is ready for snuffing out the *star*, the performance is at eight this evening. Fine, but first I have to get there.

The road stretches through woodlands, then crawls into the taiga. We ride silently. Pines, firs, and deciduous trees surround us, heavy with snow. But the sun is already heading toward sunset. Another hour or so and it will be dark. We drive about ten versts. Our Zhu-Ba-Ze turns onto a snow-covered country road.

My city Mercedov would get stuck right away. But the Boar couldn't care less—the one-and-a-half-arshin tires chew up the snow like a meat grinder. The Chinese boar barges through the Russian snow. We continue on for a verst, then another, and a third. And the age-old taiga suddenly opens. We've arrived! A fantastical tower rises over a wide clearing; it's built of ancient pines, has fanciful turrets, latticework windows, carved window casings, a copper-tiled roof, and is topped with a weather cock. The tower is surrounded by a ten-arshin pike fence made of incredibly thick logs sharpened at the top. Neither man nor beast could crawl over those pikes. Perhaps the stone Yermak Timofeevich might try, but even he would scrape his granite balls.

We drive up to the plank gates coated in forged iron. The Zhu-Ba-Ze sends an invisible, inaudible signal. The bolts slide back. We drive into the courtyard of Praskovia's estate. Guards in Chinese attire surround the car with swords and cudgels. All the clairvoyant's inner guards are Chinese, masters of kung fu. I get out of the Boar and climb the steps of the carved entrance, decorated with Siberian animals carved out of wood. All the beasts here exist in loving harmony. It's not a portico, but a wonder of wonders! Here you have a lynx licking a roe deer's forehead, wolves playing with a boar, hares kissing foxes, and grouse sitting on an ermine. Two bears support the pillars of the doorway.

I enter.

Inside everything is totally different. Here there's nothing carved, Russian. Smooth, bare walls of marble, a granite floor illuminated green from below, a ceiling of black wood. Lamps burn, incense smokes. A waterfall streams down a marble wall, white lilies float in a pool.

The clairvoyant's servants approach me silently. Like shadows from the afterlife, their hands are cool, their faces impenetrable. They take my weapons, mobilov, caftan, jacket, hat, and boots. I stand there in my shirt, pants, and goat-wool socks. I stretch my arms back. The noiseless servants dress me in a silk Chinese robe, button the cloth-covered buttons, and give me soft slippers. That's the way it is for everyone who comes here. Counts, princes, lords of the capital from the Inner Circle—all change into robes when they visit the clairvoyant.

I pass into the interior of the house. As always, it's empty and quiet. Chinese vases and beasts chiseled out of stone stand in the dim light. Chinese characters recalling wisdom and eternity adorn the walls.

A Chinese voice speaks:

"Missus awaits you near the fire."

That means we'll talk near the fireplace. She likes to carry on conversations in front of the fire. Or maybe she's just freezing? Staring at a fire is a great pleasure, though. As our Batya says, there are three things you want to look at continuously: fire, the sea, and other people's work.

The silent guards lead me into the fireplace chamber. It's dusky in here, quiet. The only sound is the logs burning, crackling in the wide fireplace. And it's not only logs, but books as well. Books mixed in with birch wood, as always at the clairvoyant's. Next to the fireplace there's a pile of logs and a pile of books. I wonder what the clairvoyant is burning today? The last time it was poetry.

The doors open, I hear a rustle. She's here.

I turn. The clairvoyant Praskovia moves toward me on her invariable shiny blue crutches, dragging her emaciated legs along the floor, staring at me with her immobile but cheerful eyes. Russ, rush, rustle. That's her legs sliding across the granite. That's her *sound*.

"Hello, dovey."

"Hello, Praskovia Mamontovna."

She moves smoothly, as though she were sliding on ice skates. She comes quite close and stops. I look into her face. Unusual, it is. There's not another one like it in all Russia. It isn't female and it isn't male, neither old nor young, neither sad nor happy, neither evil nor kind. Her green eyes are always cheery. But this cheeriness is not for us, simple mortals, to understand. Only God knows what stands behind them.

"You flew in?"

"I flew in, Praskovia Mamontovna."

"Sit down."

I sit in an armchair in front of the fireplace. She lowers herself onto her chair of dark wood. She nods to the servant. He picks up a book from the pile and tosses it on the fire.

"The same old business?"

"The very same."

"The old is like a stone in water. Fish splash around the stone, above the sky birds fly, in the white air playing high, birds long-winded, like people intended. People spin and turn, but never return. Their life is civil, but they gibber-jabber drivel, they topple in waves, surround themselves with graves, retreat far into the earth, from women again are birthed."

She falls silent and stares at the fire. I stare quietly, too. A kind of shyness overtakes the soul when you're with her. I'm not as shy with His Majesty as I am before Praskovia.

"You brought hair again?"

"I did."

"And the shirt?"

"I brought the undershirt as well, Praskovia Mamontovna."

"The shirt that's under is always asunder, smarter ever after, avoids disaster, sours, turns baldish, in the wash is scalded; once dried and smooth, from beloved don't remove, pressed to the skin, good will in the end."

She stares into the fire. Fyodor Mikhailovich Dostoevsky's *Idiot* is burning. It started with the ends, now the cover is smoking. The clairvoyant again signals the servant. He tosses another book on the fire: Lev Nikolaevich Tolstoy's *Anna Karenina*; it lies there awhile, then suddenly flares. I watch, bewitched.

"What you looking at? You never burned books?"

"We burn only harmful books, Praskovia Mamontovna. Obscene and subversive books."

"And you think these are useful?"

"The Russian classics are helpful to the state."

"Dovey, books should only be practical: about carpentry, stove-building, contracting, electricity, shipbuilding, mechanical engineering, artificial hearing, on weaving and sheaving, on casting and basting, on foundries on boundaries, on plastic and mastic."

I don't argue with her. I'm wary. She is always right. If she's angry she can easily throw you out by the scruff without a second thought. And I have important business to take care of.

"Why so quiet?"

"What . . . should I say?"

"Well, tell me what's going on in Moscow?"

I know that the clairvoyant's home has no news bubbles and no radio. That's first of all. And second—she doesn't like us, oprichniks. But then she's not alone in that. And thank God . . .

"In Moscow life is good, the people live and prosper, there are no rebellions, a new underground highway is being built between Savelevsky Station and Domodedovo—"

"I'm not talking about that, dovey," she interrupts me. "How many people did you kill today? I can tell—you smell like fresh blood."

"We suppressed one noble."

She looks at me intently and speaks:

"Suppressed one, but took out ten. Blood never covers blood. Blood in blood ends. Weary is the ending, sweat it out—then comes mending. What heals with scabs will turn to rags, crack and burst, in new blood birthed."

Again she stares into the fire. You can't figure her out: last time she almost kicked me out when she heard that six clerks from the Trade Department had been *whipped* on Lobnoe Mesto in Red Square. She hissed that we were *dark* bloodsuckers. And the time before that, learning about the execution of the Far Eastern general, she said it wasn't enough . . .

"Your monarch is a white birch. On that birch there's a dry branch. And on that branch is a black kite, pecking a live squirrel in the back; the squirrel gnashes its teeth—if you listen with a pure ear, you can make out two words in that screak: 'key' and 'east.' Understand, dovey?"

I remain silent. She's allowed to say anything. She hits me on the forehead with her wizened hand.

"Think!"

What's there to think about? You can think and think and you still won't understand a damn thing.

"What fits between these words?"

"I don't know, Praskovia Mamontovna. Maybe . . . a hollow trunk?"

"You've got a sorrowful excuse for a brain, dovey. Not a hollow tree, but Russia."

That's what it is . . . Russia. Since it's Russia, I lower my eyes to the floor at once. I look at the fire. And see *The Idiot* and *Anna Karenina* in flames. I have to say—they burn well. In general, books burn well. Manuscripts go like gunpowder. I've seen many book and manuscript bonfires—in our *courtyard*, and in the Secret Department. For that matter the Writers' Chamber itself burned quite a bit on Manezh Square, purging itself of its own subversive writers, thereby cutting our workload. One thing I can say for sure—they always make for a special fire. It's a *warm* fire. It was even warmer eighteen years ago when people burned their foreign-travel passports on Red Square. Now that was an enormous fire! It made a strong impression on me, since I was an adolescent at the time. In January there was a deep freeze, but at His Majesty's call people brought their foreign-travel passports to the main square of the country and tossed them into the fire. They kept bringing them and bringing them. From other cities they came to Moscow, the capital, to burn the legacy of the White Troubles. They came to take an oath to His Majesty. That fire burned nearly two months . . .

I glance at the clairvoyant. Her green eyes are fixed on the fire, everything forgotten. She's sitting there like an Egyptian mummy. But business won't wait. I cough.

She stirs:

"When did you last drink milk?"

I try to remember:

"The day before yesterday at breakfast. But I never drink milk separately, Praskovia Mamontovna. I use it with coffee."

"Don't drink cow's milk. Only eat cow's butter. You know why?"

I don't know anything, for crying out loud.

"Cow's milk at the bedstead sings: in the heart I'll sit fast, poison amass, blend with water, with myself swaddle, pray to the calf, my other half, the calf's bones come home, do nothing but moan, bones of white, lazybones smite. They'll thunder, expire, sink your strength in the mire."

I nod.

"I won't. I won't drink any milk."

She takes my hand with her bony but soft hand:

"But eat butter. Because cow's butter strength does utter, gathers churning all 'round turning, forms a ball, falls in the hall, fat delivers, enters the liver, spreads under the skin, strength bringing in."

I nod. I like cow's butter. Especially on hot rolls, with a bit of beluga caviar . . .

"Well, let's hear your business."

I reach into my inner pocket and take out the blue silk pouch embroidered with Her Highness's initials. I draw a man's under-shirt of the finest make from the pouch, and, in a piece of folded paper, two locks of hair: one black and the other fair. Praskovia takes the hair first. She places it on her left palm, runs her fingers through it, examines it, moves her lips, and asks:

"His name?"

"Mikhail."

She whispers something over the hair, mixes the two locks together, squeezes them in her fist. Then she orders:

"The basin!"

Her almost identical servants stir. They bring a clay bowl with cedar oil, place it on the clairvoyant's knees. She throws the hair in the oil, takes the bowl in her bony hands, and lifts it to her face. Then she begins:

"Stick like glue and dry, for ageless ages, the heart of the goodfellow Mikhail to the heart of the beauty Tatyana. Stick like glue and dry. Stick like glue and dry. Stick like glue and dry. Stick like glue and dry. Stick like glue and dry."

Praskovia takes the shirt of the young lieutenant of the Kremlin regiment, Mikhail Efimovich Skoblo, and places it in the oil. Then she gives the basin back to her servants. That's it.

She turns her clairvoyant eyes to me:

"Tell Her Highness that today, close to dawn, the heart of Mikhail will adhere to her heart."

"Thank you, Praskovia Mamontovna. The money will come, as always."

"Tell them not to send me any more money. What am I supposed to do—pickle it in a barrel? Tell them to send me fern seeds, Baltic herring, and books. I've burned all of mine."

"What kind of books specifically?" I ask.

"Russian, Russian . . ."

I nod and stand. And begin to feel nervous. It wouldn't be bad to ask about my own affairs now. And you can't hide anything from Praskovia.

"What are you fidgeting about? Decided to say a word or two of your own?"

"Yes, I have, Praskovia Mamontovna."

"Don't need to open your mouth, my eagle, you're as clear as a bell: you have a girl coming up to her time."

There you go. That's it.

"Which one?"

"The one who lives in your house."

Anastasia! Good Lord. I gave her pills. Ah, the sly cunt.

"A long time?"

"More than a month. She'll have a boy."

I'm quiet, trying to take myself in hand. Well, so what . . . it happens. It can be dealt with.

"You wanted to ask about your job?"

"Well, I . . ."

"So far, everything's fine. But some are jealous."

"I know, Praskovia Mamontovna."

"So if you know, beware. Your car will break down in a week. You'll come down with something, not too bad. They'll drill through your leg. The left one. You'll get some money. Not much. You'll get hit in the mug. Not too hard."

"Who'll do it?"

"Your boss."

What a relief. Batya is like my own father. Today he'll give me a thrashing—tomorrow he'll be kind. And my leg . . . that's just the usual stuff.

"That's all, dovey. Get out of here."

All but not all. One more question. I haven't ever asked it, but today something urges me to ask. A serious frame of mind. I screw up my courage.

"So what else do you want?" Praskovia looks at me steadily.

"What will happen to Russia?"

She doesn't answer, but looks at me carefully.

I wait with *trepidation*.

"It'll be all right."

I bow, touching the stone floor with my right hand.

And I leave.

The flight back isn't bad, although there are more people in the plane. I drink Yermak beer, chew on salted peas, watch a film about our valiant moneychangers from the Treasury. How they fought with China Union Pay four years ago. It was a stormy time. The Chinese wanted to grab us by the throat again, but things didn't work out for the slant-eyes. The Treasury held on, and responded with the second mintage. New coins sparkled with Russian gold in those slanted eyes. *Diao da lian!** Friendship is friendship, as they say, but Treasury tobacco is something else altogether.

It's evening in Moscow.

I drive from Vnukovo Airport into the city, and turn on the enemy radio.

My loyal Mercedov finds the Swedish radio station Paradigm, for our underground intellectuals. It's a major resource, seven channels. I run through the channels. Today they're having an anniversary program: "The Russian Cultural Underground." All stuff that's twenty or even thirty years old. It's meant to let our senile bloody fifth column shed some tears.

---

* No fucking way! (*Chin.*).

The first channel is broadcasting a book by someone named Rykunin, *Where Did Derrida Dine?* It has detailed descriptions of the places the Western philosopher ate during his visit to post-Soviet Moscow. One of the most important chapters is called "Leftovers of the Great." The second channel is marking the twenty-fifth anniversary of the exhibition "Caution, Religion!" Some old lady who participated in the legendary obscurantist exhibition is being awarded a medal for being a "Victim of the Russian Orthodox Church." In a trembling little voice the old bag reminisces, babbling on about "the bearded barbarians in cassocks, bursting in and obliterating our beautiful, honorable, authentic works of art." On the third channel there's a discussion between Vipperstein and Onufrienko about cloning the genre of the Great Rotten Novel, about the behavioral model of Sugary Buratino, and about medhermeneutical adultery. On the fourth, some Igor Pavlovich Tikhy speaks seriously about the "Negation of a Negation of Negation of a Negation" in A. Shestigorsky's novel *The Ninth Wife*. On the fifth, Borukh Gross's bass voice babbles about America, which has become the subconscious of China, and about China, now the subconscious of Russia, and about Russia, which has still not become even its own subconscious. The sixth channel is given over to the puppies of a man-dog, a well-known "artist" in the years of the White Troubles. The puppies are howling something about "freedom of corporeal discourse." And finally, the seventh channel of this stinking radio station is permanently relegated to the poetry of Russian minimalism and con-sep-chew-a-lism . . . In a gloom-and-doom voice, Vsevolod Nekros reads his verse, which consists mostly of coughs, quacks, and interjections:

"boo, buck, bod,
there you have God.

bek, bud, bok,
there you have Bach.
piff, paff, pof,
now you've got a Crotch.
And that's quite enough."

Hmmm. What can you say? Our underground intellectuals feed on this dung, this vomit, this deafening emptiness. Hideous polyps they are, growing on the body of our healthy Russian art. "Minimalism," "paradigm," "discourse," "CON-SEP-CHEW-A-LISM" . . . From early childhood I've heard these words. But I still don't understand what they mean. But take the painting *Boyarina Morozova*, now—just as I got to know it when I was five years old, I know it to this very day. All this "contemporary" art isn't worth one brushstroke of our great artist Surikov. When my soul feels low, when the enemy overwhelms us, when crafty circles begin to close in—you can run into the Tretiakov Gallery for a minute, visit the great canvas, and see: the sleigh with the unruly boyarina drives over the Russian snow, the boy runs, the village idiot, ready to cross himself, raises his two fingers, the coachman grins . . . Russia explodes from the wall. So intensely you'll forget about the meaningless bustle of the world. Your lungs inhale Russian air. That's all you need. And thank God . . .

The whips crack: it's Prima Kozlova calling.

"Andrei Danilovich, I have the money."

That's good. We set a place, and meet near the People's Library. I pick up a leather bag stuffed with coins of the first mintage. The first will do just as well.

I drive along Mokhovaya Street.

Across from the old university I notice a flogging is about to take place. Interesting. I slow down and pull over. This is where they flog the intelligentsia. Manezh Square, a bit farther on, is usually for the Zemstvos; Lobnoe Mesto is for clerks. The Streltsy flog themselves in the garrisons. All sorts of other scum are *steamed* at Smolensk Square, Miusskaya Square, on the Mozhaisk highway, and at the market in Yasenevo.

As I drive up, I lower the window and light up a cigarette. People part so that I can see better: they respect the oprichniks. Shka Ivanov—a well-known executioner of the Moscow intelligentsia—stands on the wooden platform. On Mondays he always does the flogging here. The people know him and respect him. Shka Ivanov is big, stocky, has white skin, a broad chest, curly hair, and wears round eyeglasses. He reads the sentence in a booming voice. I listen with half an ear, and look around at the crowd. As far as I can figure out, some junior clerk, Danilkov, from the Literary Chamber is to be flogged for "criminal negligence." He copied something important the wrong way, screwed it up, and then hid it. An educated crowd mills around, a lot of students, upper-school girls. Shka Ivanov rolls up the sentence, sticks it in his pocket, and whistles. His assistant appears— Mishanya the Quotationer. He's a tall, narrow-shouldered, shaven-headed beanpole with an eternally mocking expression on his face. He got his nickname because he says everything as if it's in quotation marks. After every word, he raises his hands to his temples and makes his "quotation marks," at which point he strongly resembles a gray hare. Mishanya brings the convicted Danilkov out on a chain: he's an ordinary junior clerk with a long nose. He crosses himself, muttering something.

Mishanya speaks to him in a loud voice:

"Now, townsman, we're going to thrash you!"

And right away, he makes those quotation marks with his fingers.

"We'll give you a real beaut of a thrashing!"

And again, the quotation marks. People laugh and applaud.

Students whistle. The torturers grab the junior clerk and tie him down. Shka Ivanov grins:

"Lie down, lie down, you fucking fruit!"

Executioners and army elders in Russia are allowed to curse. His Majesty exempted them in recognition of their difficult professions.

Danilkov is tied down; Mishanya sits on his legs and pulls down his pants. Judging by the scars, the junior clerk's ass has been flogged more than once. So this isn't the first time Danilkov has been *steamed*. The students whistle and hoot.

"So you see, friend," Mishanya says, "literature ain't some sort of motorcycle!"

Shka Ivanov swings the knout and begins to flog him. He does it so well that you get carried away watching. He knows his job, this butcher does, he loves it. The people respect him for work well done. The whip strolls across the junior clerk's ass: first from the left, then from the right. A neat grate forms on the ass. Danilkov screams and wails; his long nose turns purple.

But it's time to go. I flick my cigarette butt to a beggar, and turn onto Tverskaya. I'm heading for the concert hall on Strastnoi Boulevard. The *star*'s performance is already coming to an end. On my way, I get in touch with the Good Fellows and get the details. They seem to have everything ready. I park the car, and enter by the service door. One of the Good Fellow underlings meets me and escorts me to the auditorium. I sit in the fourth row, on the aisle.

The *star* is on stage. A people's storyteller, bard, and epic tale spinner, Savely Ivanovich Artamonov—or, as the people call him, Artamosha. Gray-haired, white-bearded, stately, with a handsome face, though he isn't young. He sits on his usual fake bench in a black silk peasant shirt with his usual saw in hand. Artamosha runs his bow across the saw—and the saw sings in a delicate voice, bewitching the hall. Under the enchantment of the whine Artamosha continues reciting-singing another of his *bylinas* in a deep, chesty, unhurried voice:

"Look, our Fox, our Sly one, our lovely Patrikeevna, ay ay is me,
Has come to the Kremlin, to the Kremlin's low kennel, oh woe is
    me ay ay . . .
The kennel built of mighty logs, ay ay.
All the kennel windows are teeny-tiny, ay ay.
All the grates are closed, ay ay.
The kennel doors are thick and oak,
Locked with ten-ton locks and bolts, lovey-dovey mine . . ."

Artamosha throws back his white head, squeezes his eyes shut, and rolls his stately shoulders. His saw sings. The people in the auditorium are all *worked up*—toss a match and they'll explode. Artamosha's old fans are in the first rows, swaying in time to the saw, wailing along. In the middle of the auditorium, some half-witted woman is moaning a lament. In the back rows they're sniffling and someone mutters angrily. A difficult audience. How the Good Fellows are going to work here is beyond me.

"Now how shall you open the bolts and locks, Mama dearest?
How shall you unblock the locks and slide the oak, Grandmama
    dear?
How shall you climb and clamber through the window, my baby
    bunting?
How shall you dig, my dear little lamb?"

I glance at the audience out of the corner of my eye and look around: the Good Fellows have sat themselves in the center. Obviously the Artamonov followers wouldn't let them in the first rows. Judging by the quantity of Good Fellow mugs, it seems they decided to take over with numbers, like they usually do. God grant. We'll keep an eye out, we'll see . . .

"She coughs, our Fox, our sly Patrikeevna, she coughs up and
    up, ay ay,
A key of gold she vomits up,
To open the ten-ton cast-iron lock,
To open the door of oak, ay ay,
She creeps through the kennel, through the Kremlin,
To the hounds in the dark, in the deep,"

The audience begins to sing along: "To the hounds! To the hounds! To the hounds!" The first rows begin to toss and sway; in the back behind they're shouting, crying, lamenting. Near me a richly dressed fat lady crosses herself, sings and sways. Artamosha plays his saw, his head thrown back so far you can see his Adam's apple.

"To the hounds dreaming nose to tail, the hounds so sound
    asleep,
To the hounds well-fed and sleek.
To the hounds so lean, the hounds so young and keen.
She comes to trifle and to fiddle with them, bringing her wanton,
    whorish fiddling!
Plucking at them to do it, ay ay.
She fiddles and plucks, ay ay, to sate her filthy . . ."

Just a tiny bit more, and the hall will erupt. I feel like I'm sitting on a powder keg. But the Good Fellows keep quiet, the muttonheads . . .

"Then the hounds awake, ay ay ay,
Then the hounds wag the sleep from their eyes, ay ay . . ."

Artamosha opens his eyes, pauses, and scans the audience intently. His saw howls.

"How they throw themselves upon our Fox, upon our Sly Patri-
      keevna!
How they fuck her in the kennel!
Full of canine excrement!
In the corner, in the stinking corner!
And she's delighted!
More, come on, more of you!
Hotter, quicker, more!
It won't be too much for me!
I'll satisfy you all!
I'm ready for anything!
I have no shame!
All my hounds!
All my hounds!
All my lovely hounds!"

Artamosha's shout is hoarse, his saw squeals. The hall explodes. In the first rows there are cries: "Let her have it! The bitch!
That's right, the shameless harpy!" Some cross themselves and
spit, others wail, some sing along, "All my hounds!" And then,
finally, the captain of the Good Fellows, a guy nicknamed Khobot, stands up and throws a rotten tomato at Artamosha. The
vegetable hits the bard in the chest. As if by command, all the
other Good Fellows stand in the middle of the hall and launch a
hail of tomatoes at Artamosha. In a moment the bard is covered
in red.

The audience gasps.

And Khobot roars so loud that his kind face turns crimson:
"Ooobsceeene!!! Slander against Her Highness!!!"

The Good Fellows, following up Khobot:

"Slander! Subversion! Work and Word!"

The audience freezes. I freeze, too. Artamosha sits on his bench drenched in tomatoes. Suddenly he raises his hand. He stands. His look quiets the Good Fellows like a command. Only Khobot tries to shout "Slander!" but his voice is alone. I already know—they've lost. It's a disaster.

"There they are, the Kremlin hounds!" Artamosha says in a loud voice, pointing toward the center of the audience with a red finger.

A sort of atomic explosion takes place in the hall: everyone attacks the Good Fellows. They clobber them, beat the living daylights out of them. The Good Fellows defend themselves, they fight back, but in vain. The stupid idiots sat in the center to boot, so they've ended up surrounded. They're flattened on all sides. Artamosha stands on the stage covered in tomatoes, like some kind of dripping red St. George the Dragonslayer. The fat lady near me shrieks and pushes toward the thick of things:

"Hounds! Hounds!"

Clear enough. I rise. And leave.

In our difficult and important work things don't always turn out right. My fault this time—I didn't instruct them, didn't keep an eye on them. Didn't anticipate or warn them. Well, there was no time—I was fighting for the Road. That's how I justify it to Batya. When it's over I want to drop by to see Khobot, and bop him on the head, but I feel sorry for him—he's had enough for one day. From the people.

Hmmm . . . Artamosha sure gets them worked up. But he's playing with fire. He's gone overboard. Gone so far that it's time to *snuff* him out. The scoundrel began as a genuine bard. At first he sang traditional Russian epics. About the deeds of Ilya Muromets, Buslai, Solovei Budimirovich. He became famous all across New Rus. Made a good living. Set himself up with two houses. Acquired high-placed patrons. He could have gone on living and living, wallowing in his popularity, but no—something got into him. He began to sing exposés of morals and manners. Not just of anyone, but of Her Highness. As they say, you couldn't fall higher. And Her Highness . . . well, that's a whole story in itself. A bitter one.

To take the broad view, the state's point of view, His Majesty had a stroke of bad luck. In fact, he didn't have any luck. Big time. The one blotch in our New Russia is His Majesty's spouse. And you can't wash this spot away, or cover it up, or remove it. You can only wait, be patient, and hope . . .

Whistle-blow-moan.

The red signal on my mobilov.

Her Highness!

Speak of the devil, God forgive me . . . She always calls as soon as I start thinking about her. It's downright mystical! I cross myself, turn to answer the phone, and, bowing my head:

"Yes, Your Highness."

I see her plump, willful face, with a little mustache above crimson, carnivorous lips:

"Komiaga! Where are you?"

Her voice is chesty, deep. You can see that our *mama* has just woken up. Her eyes are pretty, black, with velvet eyelashes. These eyes always shine with a powerful fire.

"I'm driving around Moscow, Your Highness."

"You saw Praskovia?"

"Yes, Your Highness. I did everything you asked."

"Why aren't you reporting to me?"

"Forgive me, Your Highness, I just flew in."

"Well buzz yourself over here on the double. Fast as a fly."

"I hear and obey, Your Highness."

Back to the Kremlin again. I turn onto Miasnitskaya Street, and it's jam-packed—it's evening, rush hour, of course. I turn on my State Snarl and cars part in front of my Mercedov with the dog's head; I steadily make my way to Lubianskaya Square, and there I stop dead: a traffic-fucking-jam, God forgive me. I'll have to wait.

A powdery snow falls, dusting the cars. And as before on Lubianskaya our Maliuta stands tall, bronze, stooped, preoccupied; powdered with snow, he stares out intently from beneath his overhanging eyebrows. In his time there weren't any traffic jams. There were only fruit jams . . .

On the Children's World department store building there's an enormous frame with a live advertisement: for Sviatogor flannel leggings. A curly-headed youth sits on a bench; a beauty of a girl in a traditional Russian headdress kneels down in front of him with new leggings in her hands. The young man extends his bare leg to the strum of a balalaika and the sobs of a harmonica. The young lady wraps it in the leggings, and pulls on his boot. A voice declares:

"Sviatogor Trading Company leggings. Your foot will feel like it's in a cradle." Right away you hear a lullaby, and see a wicker cradle rocking gently with legging-wrapped legs in it: rock-a-bye baby . . . And the girl's voice says: "They'll cradle your legs!"

Suddenly I'm feeling kind of sad . . . I turn on Radio Rus video channel and order a "minute of Russian poetry." A slightly nervous young man declaims:

"The fields flow with fog,
Bark and birch are injured,
The ground's a bare black bog,
Spring's not icumen in.
The birch bark's been bled
With a jagged axe blade,
Down, down the sap runs,
Calling to matins."

One of the new poets. Not bad, it creates a certain mood . . . One thing I don't get, though: how does birch sap call to matins? Church bells should call to matins. Up ahead I notice a traffic cop in a fluorescent coat. I call him on the government line:

"Officer! Clear the road for me!"

Together—he with a baton, I with the State Snarl—we clear the way. I turn onto Ilyinka, make my way down Rybny and Varvarka streets to Red Square, drive in through the Spassky Gates, and race to Her Highness's residence. I drop the car with the doorkeepers in raspberry-colored caftans, and run up the granite steps. The guards, who wear gilded livery, open the first door for me. I fly into the pink marble lobby, stop before the second door—a transparent one that shines weakly. This door is one ray from the ceiling to the floor. Two lieutenants of the Kremlin regiment stand on either side, and look straight through me. I catch my breath, clear my thoughts, and walk through the shining door. It's impossible to hide anything from this broad ray—neither weapons, nor poison, nor any evil design.

I set foot in Her Highness's residence.

A stately assistant meets me with a bow:

"Her Highness awaits you."

She leads me through the residence, through countless rooms and halls. The doors open by themselves, noiselessly. They close just as quietly. Finally—the lilac bedroom of our lady, Her Highness. I enter. Before me on a wide lounge bed is His Majesty's spouse.

I bend over in a long bow to the ground.

"Hello, murderer."

That's what she calls all of us oprichniks. But not with reproach, with *humor*.

"The best of health to you, Your Highness Tatyana Alekseevna."

I raise my eyes. Her Highness reclines in a nightgown of violet silk that goes with the tender lilac color of the bedroom. Her black hair is in slight disarray, it falls over her large shoulders. Her down comforter is thrown aside. On the bed is a Japanese fan, Chinese nephrite balls for rolling in your fingers, a gold mobilov, a sleeping greyhound named Katerina, and Darya Adashkovaya's book *Pernicious Pugs*. In her plump white hands Her Highness holds a gold snuffbox, strewn with diamond pustules. She takes a pinch of tobacco from the snuffbox, and stuffs it up her nostril. She freezes. Her moist black eyes look at me. Then she sneezes. So hard that the lilac pendants on the chandelier quiver.

"Oh, my God, I am going to die." Her Highness throws her head back on four pillows.

The assistant wipes her nose with a cambric handkerchief, and brings her a shot of cognac. Without this Her Highness's morning doesn't begin. And her morning is our evening.

"Tanya, the bath!"

The assistant comes out. Her Highness has a bite of lemon with her cognac, and stretches her hand out to me. I grab her weighty arm. Leaning on me, she rises from the lounge bed. She claps her heavy hands, and heads for the lilac door. It opens. Her Highness floats into the room. In body she's portly, tall, stately. God certainly provided her ample volumes of white flesh.

Standing in the bed chamber, my gaze follows Her Wide Highness.

"Why'd you stop? Come in here."

I submissively follow her into the spacious white marble bathroom. Here two other helpers are bustling about, preparing the bath, opening champagne. Her Highness takes a thin glass, then sits down on the toilet. That's what she always does—first a bit of cognac, then some champagne. Her Highness does her business, sipping from the champagne glass. Then she stands up:

"Well, why aren't you talking? Tell me about it."

She raises her white arms. In a twinkling the helpers take off her nightgown. I lower my eyes, but manage once more to notice how buxom and white-skinned is Her Highness. Oy, there's not another like . . . She descends the marble steps into her filled bathtub. She sits down.

"Your Highness, I followed your instructions. Praskovia said it would be tonight. She did everything correctly."

Her Highness is quiet. She drinks her champagne. Sighs. So hard that the bubbles in the bath flutter.

"Tonight?" she asks again. "That's . . . your nighttime?"

"Our nighttime, Your Highness."

"I think that means . . . lunchtime. All right."

She sighs again. Finishes off the glass of champagne. They give her another.

"What did the clairvoyant ask for?"

"Baltic herring, fern seeds, and books."

"Books?"

"Yes. For the fireplace."

"Ah . . . yes . . ."

Her main assistant enters without knocking:

"Your Highness, the children have come."

"Already? Bring them in."

The assistant leaves and returns with the ten-year-old twins—Andriusha and Agafia. They dash in and run to their mother. Her Highness rises from the bath, baring herself to the waist, covering her *enormously wide* breasts. The children kiss her on the cheek:

"Good morning, Mamochka!"

She embraces them without letting go of her champagne glass.

"Good morning, my dears. I'm running a bit late today, I thought we would breakfast together."

"Mama, we already had dinner!" Andriusha shouts and slaps the water.

"Well, that's wonderful," she says, wiping the spray of foam from her face.

"Mamulya, I won at Go Ze.* I found the *bao xian*.†"

"*Hao hai zi*.‡" Her Highness kisses her daughter. "*Min min*.§"

Her Highness's Chinese is really rather old-fashioned . . .

"And *I* won at Go Ze a long time ago!" Andriusha says, splashing water on his sister.

"*Sha gua!*¶" Agafia splashes back.

"Gashenka, Andriusha . . ." Her Highness frowns, furrowing her beautiful black eyebrows, and covering her breast as before. She immerses herself in her bath. "Where's Papa?"

"Papa's with the armies," says Andriusha, pulling a toy pistol out of its holster and aiming at me. "Bang, baaang!"

The red target ray settles on my forehead. I smile.

"Pouff! Bang Bang!" Andriusha pulls the trigger and a tiny ball hits me in the forehead.

It bounces off.

I smile at the future heir to the Russian state.

"Where is His Majesty?" Her Highness asks the tutor standing just outside the door.

"At army headquarters, Your Highness. Today is the anniversary of the Andreev Corps."

"So that means there's no one to breakfast with me . . ." Her Highness sighs, taking another glass of champagne from the gold tray. "All right, go on all of you . . ."

The children, servant, and I head for the door.

"Komiaga!"

I turn around.

"Have breakfast with me."

"At your service, Your Highness."

---

* A Chinese 4-D game that became popular in New Russia after the well-known events of November 2027.
† Shield (*Chin.*).
‡ Attaboy (*Chin.*).
§ Splendid (*Chin.*).
¶ Fool (*Chin.*).

I await Her Highness in the small dining room. An *unprecedented* honor has been bestowed on me—to share the morning meal with our lady. Her Highness usually breakfasts in the evening, if not with His Majesty, then with someone from the Inner Circle—Countess Borisova or Princess Volkova. With her many "guests" and hangers-on she only lunches. And that is already far after midnight. Her Highness always dines at sunrise.

I sit at the breakfast table, which is already set: adorned with white roses, and laid with gold dishes and crystal. Four servants in silvery emerald caftans stand by the walls.

Forty minutes have already passed, but Her Highness isn't here yet. She spends a long time on her morning toilette. I sit and think about our lady. She has a hard time of it, for many reasons. Not only because of natural feminine *weaknesses*. But because of blood. Her Highness is a half-Jewess. There's no way around it. That's partly why so many pasquinades are written about her, why so much gossip and rumor is spread about her around Moscow and all of Russia, for that matter.

I've never had a problem with Jews. My departed father wasn't a kike eater either. He told me that people used to say that anyone who played the violin more than ten years automatically became a Jew. Mama, may she rest in peace for eternity, didn't have any problems with Jews; she said it wasn't the Yids that were dangerous for Russia, but the pseudo-Jews, people whose blood was Russian but pretended to be kikes. When I didn't want to study German as an adolescent, my mathematician grandfather would recite a little poem he wrote, a parody of the famous Soviet poet Mayakovsky.*

Were I
    A Jew
        Late in life,
Even then—
    Nicht zweifelnd und bitter†
I'd learn
    German
            If only because,
'Twas German spoken
            by Hitler.

But not all were such Jew lovers as my relatives. Outbursts did occur, yes, and Judaic blood was spilled on Russian land. All of this smoldered and dragged on right up until His Majesty's "Decree On Russian Orthodox Names." This decree required all Russian citizens who were not christened in the Orthodox faith to have non-Orthodox names: they had to have names corresponding to their ethnicity. After that many of our Borises became Borukhs; Viktors—Agvidors; and Levs—Leibs. That's how Our Sage Majesty resolved the Jewish question in Russia once and for all. He took all the smart Jews under his wing. The

---

* "Were I even a Negro late in my life, even so, without dawdling or dreariness, I'd go and learn Russian simply because, 'twas in Russian that Lenin conversed."
† Without doubt or bitterness.

dimwitted ones scattered. It quickly became obvious that Jews were really quite useful to the Russian government. They were irreplaceable in treasury, trade, and ambassadorial affairs.

The problem with Her Highness was different. This wasn't a matter of the Jewish question. The question was the purity of blood. Had our lady Her Highness been half Tatar or Chechen it would have been the same problem. There's no getting around it. And thank God . . .

The white doors open, the greyhound Katerina bounds into the little dining room, sniffs me, barks twice and sneezes like dogs do, and jumps up on her chair. I stand and watch the open door with the motionless servants on each side. Sedate, assured steps are coming closer, building up, and—in a rustle of dark blue silk Her Highness appears in the doorway. She's large, wide, stately. Her fan is folded in her strong hand. Her luxuriant hair is pulled back, coiffed, held with gold combs, iridescent with precious stones. On Her Highness's neck is a velvet ring with the "Padishah" diamond, bordered with sapphires. Her face is powdered, she wears lipstick on her sensual lips, and her deep eyes shine under her black eyelashes.

"Sit down," she says with a wave of her fan, while she sits in the chair the servant has moved up for her.

I sit. The servant brings in a small shell with finely chopped dove meat and sets it in front of Katerina. The greyhound devours the meat, and Her Highness strokes her on the back.

"Eat up now, my little oyster."

The servants bring in a gold carafe of red wine, and fill Her Highness's glass. She picks it up in her large hand and says:

"What will you drink with me?"

"Whatever you say, Your Highness."

"Oprichniks should drink vodka. Pour him some vodka!"

They pour vodka into a crystal glass for me. Silently the servants place the *zakuski* on the table: beluga caviar, snakeroot,

Chinese mushrooms, Japanese soba noodles on ice, boiled rice, vegetables stewed in spices.

I raise my glass and stand, terribly nervous:

"To your health, Your H-h-h-high-highness . . ."

I am tongue-tied with emotion: this is the first time in my life I've sat at Her Highness's table.

"Sit down." She waves her fan, and takes a swallow from her wineglass.

I gulp the vodka down and sit. I sit like a stuffed dummy. I didn't expect to feel so shy. I'm not as shy in front of His Majesty as I am with Her Highness. And besides, I'm not exactly the most bashful of oprichniks . . .

Her Highness eats her hors d'oeuvres unhurriedly, paying me no mind.

"What's new in the capital?"

I shrug my shoulders:

"Nothing in particular, Your Highness."

"And not in particular?"

Her black eyes stare steadily at me. You can't hide from them.

"Nothing not in particular either. Well, we suppressed a noble."

"Kunitsyn? I know, I saw."

Probably as soon as Her Highness wakes up they bring her a news bubble. What else would you expect? It's government business . . .

"What else?" she asks, spreading beluga caviar on rye toast.

"Well . . . you know . . . somehow . . ." I mumble.

She stares at me.

"How did you bungle Artamosha?"

So that's what it is. She knows this, too. I inhale deeply.

"Your Highness, it's my fault."

She looks at me attentively:

"That was well put. If you'd tried to dump the whole thing

on the Good Fellows, I would have ordered you flogged right here and now. Right here."

"Forgive me, Your Highness. I was late due to other affairs, and didn't get there in time. I wasn't able to forestall events."

"It happens," she says, biting off a piece of toast with caviar and washing it down with wine. "Eat."

Thank God. There are better things to do in my position than just to keep quiet. I grab some snakeroot, put it in my mouth, follow it with a piece of rye bread. Her Highness chews, sipping wine. And then she suddenly laughs nervously, puts down her glass, and stops chewing. I stop, too.

She eyes me intently:

"Tell me, Komiaga, why do they hate me so much?"

I inhale deeply. And exhale. What can I say? And there she is, looking straight through me.

"So I love young guardsmen. So what? What difference does it make?"

Her black eyes fill with tears. She wipes them away with a handkerchief.

I pluck up my courage:

"Your Highness, it's just a handful of malicious dissenters."

She looks at me like a tigress at a mouse. I regret opening my mouth.

"It's not a handful of dissenters, you idiot. It's our barbaric people!"

I understand. The Russian people aren't easy to work with. But God hasn't given us any other people. I keep quiet. But Her Highness, forgetting about food, presses the end of her closed fan to her lips:

"They're envious because they're slaves. They know how to pretend. But they don't really love us, the powerful. And they *never* will. If they had the chance—they'd cut us to pieces."

I gather my courage again:

"Your Highness, please don't worry—we'll throttle that Artamosha. We'll squash him like a louse."

"Oh, what does Artamosha have to do with it!" She whacks her fan on the table and stands up abruptly.

I jump up immediately.

"Sit!" She waves at me.

I sit. The greyhound barks at me. Her Highness paces the dining room, her dress rustling menacingly.

"Artamosha! As if he were the problem . . ."

She walks back and forth, mumbling something to herself. She stops and tosses the fan on the table.

"Artamosha! It's the nobles' wives, they're jealous of me, they set the holy fools against me, and they in turn stir up the people. This subversive wind blows from the nobles' wives through the fools and to the people. Nikola Volokolamsky, Andriukha Zagoriansky, Afonya Ostankinsky—what kinds of things are they saying about me, huh? Well?!"

"Your Highness, these stinking curs make the rounds of the churches and spread disgusting rumors . . . But His Majesty has forbidden us to touch them . . . otherwise long ago we would have . . ."

"I'm asking you—what are they saying?!"

"Well . . . they say that at night you rub a Chinese ointment on your body, after which you turn into a dog . . ."

"And I run around with hounds! Is that it?"

"That's it, Your Highness."

"So what does Artamosha have to do with it? He's just singing rumors! Artamosha!"

She walks around, muttering angrily. Her eyes glitter. She takes her glass and drinks. She sighs:

"Hmmm . . . you ruined my appetite. All right, get out of here . . ."

I stand, bow, and walk backward, step by step.

"Wait . . ." She stops and thinks. "What was it you said Praskovia wanted?"

"Baltic herring, fern seeds, and books."

"Books. Well then, come with me. Otherwise I might forget . . ."

Her Highness quits the dining room, throwing open the doors in front of her. I try to keep up behind her. We enter the library. Her Highness's librarian jumps up and bows, a moss-covered man in glasses:

"What do you desire, Your Highness?"

"Let's go, Teryosha."

The librarian minces along after her. Her Highness goes over to the shelves. There are a lot of them. And there's a ton of books. I know that our mama likes to read from paper. And not just *Pernicious Pugs*. She's well read.

She stops. Looks at the shelves:

"This will burn well and for a long time."

She makes a sign to the librarian. He takes the collected works of Anton Chekhov off the shelves.

"Send these to Praskovia," Her Highness tells the librarian.

"Yes, ma'am." He nods, shifting the books.

"That's it!" Our mama turns and walks right out of the library.

I hurry after her. She sweeps into her quarters. The golden doors open wide, the tambourines sound, the unseen balalaika strums, and valiant voices sing.

"Go on and hit me, me-oh-mine,
A big fat stick upon my spine!
A stick that's excellent and fine.
My spine is quilted well, and lined!"

Her Highness is met by a pack of her hangers-on. They howl, squeal joyfully, and bow. There are a lot of them. All kinds: jesters, nuns well read in scripture, wandering minstrels, storytellers, *playful souls*, and *dumpling makers* crippled by science, witch doctors, masseurs, spinsters, and gingerbread men who run on electricity. "Best of the morning to you, Mamo!" all these hangers-on howl in unison.

"Good morning, my lovelies!" Her Highness smiles.

Two old jesters run up to her—Pavlusha the Hedgehog and Duga the Devil grab her by the hands, pull her along, kissing her fingers. As always, round-faced Pavlusha mutters, "Pow-yer, pow-yer, pow-yer!"

Hairy Duga grunts along:

"Eur-gasia, Eur-gasia, Eur-gasia!"

The rest begin to dance in a circle around Her Highness. I can see right off—her face grows kinder, her eyebrows calmer, her eyes no longer flash.

"How are my darlings doing here without me?"

There's wailing and whimpering in reply.

"No good, Mamo! No goooood!"

The hangers-on fall to their knees in front of Mama.

I step backward toward the exit. She notices:

"Komiaga!"

I freeze. She beckons to her chamberlain, takes a gold piece out of her purse, and tosses it to me:

"For your efforts."

I catch it, bow, and leave.

Evening. It's snowing. I am driving my Mercedov through Moscow. I hold the wheel and squeeze the gold piece in my fist. It burns my palm like burning charcoal. It's not pay, it's a *gift*. Not much money, only ten rubles, but it's dearer to me than a thousand . . .

Her Highness always creates a *storm* of feelings in my soul. Hard to describe. Like two tsunamis colliding: one wave is hatred, the other is love. I hate our mama because she shames His Majesty, undermines the people's belief in their sovereign. I love her for her character, for her strength and integrity, for her unyielding obstinacy. And for . . . her white, tender, incomparable, boundless, ample breast, which *occasionally* I manage to glimpse out of the corner of my eye, thank God. Those unexpected evening *viewings* are unlike anything else. A sidelong peep at Her Highness's breast . . . is rapture, gentlemen! One thing's a pity, though: Her Highness prefers guardsmen to oprichniks. And it's unlikely her preference will change. Well, let God be her judge.

I look at the clock: 21:42.

Today is Monday; the oprichnik repast begins at 21:00. I'm late. But it's no big deal. Our communal evening meal is at

Batya's residence on Mondays and Thursdays only. That's on Yakimanka Street, in the merchant Igumnov's house, the very same house where French ambassadors nested for nearly a century. The house has been occupied by the oprichnina since the famous events of summer 2021, when His Majesty publicly tore up the French ambassador's credentials and sent the envoy packing, having unearthed his plot to foment rebellion. No more skinny-legged Frenchmen walk there: it's our dear Batya who paces the floors in his Moroccan leather boots. Each Monday and Thursday he has dinner for all of us. The house is whimsical, it reminds you of old-time Russia as though it had deliberately been built for Batya. It was waiting until our dear Batya moved in, and it waited long enough. Thank God.

I drive up to the house. There's red all over from our Mercedovs. Like ladybugs around a piece of sugar, they've crowded around the house. I get out of the car and walk to the carved stone entrance. Batya's stern doorkeepers let me in silently. I enter, throw my caftan to the servants' waiting hands, and run down the stairs to a set of wide doors. Two guards in light-colored caftans stand by them. They bow, open the doors—and what a hubbub! The dining hall buzzes like a beehive. The sound dispels all exhaustion.

The great hall is completely full, as always. The entire Moscow oprichnina sits here. The chandeliers shine, candles burn on the table, gilded forelocks shimmer, little bells sway. Glorious! I enter with a bow to the floor, as is fit when you're late. I proceed to my place, closer to Batya. The long tables are arranged such that all abut one central table, where Batya sits with the two *wings*—the right and left. I sit down at my lawful place—fourth from Batya on the right, between Shelet and Pravda. Batya winks at me while taking a bite of a savory pie. It's no sin to be late here: we all have business to take care of, and sometimes dinner drags on till after midnight. The servant brings me a bowl of water, I wash my hands, dry them with a towel. And what do you know?—everyone's just moving on to the next course. The servants bring in Batya's grilled turkeys. And on the tables there's bread and marinated cabbage. At weekday repasts Batya doesn't care for all sorts of lavish dishes. There are carafes of wine, kvass, and springwater to drink. No vodka here on weekdays.

Pravda pours me some wine:

"So, Brother Komiaga, too many irons in the fire?"

"That's right, Brother Pravda."

I clink glasses with Pravda and Shelet, and empty my goblet in one gulp. I realize that I haven't eaten a *serious* meal in some time: with Her Highness I couldn't swallow a bite, I was so nervous. Hunger isn't a maiden—you can't treat it to a mere sturgeon-spine pie. Just in time, oh, just in time the servant places a dish with turkey, baked potatoes, and steamed turnip on the table. I pull off a turkey leg for myself, and sink my teeth into it: it's good, roasted to a T in Batya's wonderful stove. Shelet rips off a wing, and smacks his lips:

"You can't eat better anywhere than at our Batya's!"

"That's the holy truth!" Pravda belches.

"One thing's for sure," I mutter, swallowing the juicy turkey meat. "Our Batya feeds and warms us, gives us a living, and teaches us how to keep our heads on our shoulders."

Out of the corner of my eye I glance at Batya, and he, our heart and soul, senses our affection and winks while eating his meal, slowly, as always. We all feel protected by him. Thank God.

I eat, glancing at Batya's table now and then. At the edges, where the oprichnik *wings* end, honored guests sit, as is customary. Today as well: on the right is the broad-shouldered Metropolitan Kolomensky with the gray-bearded paraxyliarch of Yelokhovsky Cathedral; the ten-pood chairman of the All-Russian Society for the Observance of Human Rights wearing the badge of the Alliance of St. Michael the Archangel; smiling Father Germogen, Her Highness's spiritual adviser; some young official from the Trade Department; the trade rep of the Ukraine, Stefan Goloborodko; and Batya's old friend the entrepreneur Mikhail Trofimovich Porokhovshchikov; on the left is the oprichnina's devoted doctor, Pyotr Sergeevich Vakhrushev with his eternal assistant Bao Cai; the imposing one-eyed commander of the Kremlin regiment; the folk singer Churilo Volodevich; the inevitably disgruntled Losiuk from the Secret Department; the Russian boxing champion Zhbanov; Zakharov, the round-faced Treasury representative; Batya's game warden, Vasya Okhlobystin; the boyar Govorov; and the head Kremlin bathhouse attendant, Anton Mamona.

Batya lifts his wineglass and stands. The commotion dies down. In a stentorian voice, he proclaims:

"To His Majesty's health!"

We all stand:

"To His Majesty's health!"

We drain our glasses. Wine isn't champagne, though, you can't gulp it down. We drink slowly. We grunt, wipe our mustaches and beards, and sit down. Suddenly, like thunder from the heavens, a rainbow frame appears on the ceiling of the hall, and a painfully familiar, narrow face with a dark blond beard appears. His Majesty!

"I thank you, oprichniks!" His voice carries throughout the hall.

"Long live His Majesty!" Batya cries.

We take up the call threefold:

"Long live, long live, long live His Majesty!"

"Hail!" His Majesty answers, smiling.

"Hail! Hail!! Hail!!!" sweeps across the hall like a great wave.

We sit, lifting our faces to him. Our sun waits for us to calm down. He gazes at us warmly, with a fatherly expression:

"How was your day?"

"Work and Word! We Live to Serve, Your Majesty! Good! Thank God!"

His Majesty pauses. He looks us all over with his transparent eyes:

"I know your work. I thank you for your service. I rely on you."

"Hail!!" cries Batya.

"Hail!! Hail!!" we repeat.

The ceiling hums with our voices. His Majesty looks down from it:

"I want your advice on a certain matter."

We immediately quiet down. That's how His Majesty is: he values advice. This is his great wisdom, and his great simplicity. That's why our state flourishes under him.

We sit holding our breath.

Our Sun takes his time. Then he speaks:

"About the mortgages."

Now it's clear. We understand. The Chinese mortgages. An old problem. A tangled knot. How many times has His Majesty threatened to cut it open, and his own people got in the way, held him back. And not only *his own*, but some of us. And outsiders. And simply—others . . .

"A half hour ago I had a conversation with Zhou Shen Min. My friend, the Celestial Ruler, is concerned about the situation of the Chinese in western Siberia. You know that after I issued the decree forbidding the transfer of the local *volosts* under mortgage to the districts, things seemed to straighten out. But as it turns out, it wasn't for long. The Chinese are now getting mortgages not with the *volosts*, but with the settlements that have no landholdings under the so-called Tan Xu[*] buy-up with business petitions, so that our district officials have the right to register them as contract laborers rather than as taxed persons. They use the law On the Four Taxes. The tax collectors in the district councils, as I'm sure you realize, have been bought by them and register them not as taxpayers but as temporary hired workers with bag and baggage. And temporary workers are contract laborers according to the new regulations. It turns out that they cultivate allotments of arable land, but pay the tithe only as contract laborers, since their wives and children are listed on the shares as six-month parasites. Therefore, the district assessments of all the six-month-untaxed parasites are divided not in half, but two to three. Consequently, every six months China loses a third of its tithes. And the Tan Xu buy-up helps the Chinese living in our country to deceive their Celestial Ruler. Considering that there are twenty-eight million Chinese in western Siberia, I quite understand the concern of my friend Zhou Shen Min: China loses almost three billion yuan every six months. Today I had a conversation with Tsvetov and Zilberman. Both ministers advised me to get rid of the law On the Four Taxes."

His Majesty stops speaking. So that's what it is! Once again the tax law has stuck in the craw of one of the departmental clerks. They didn't get to share the lucre, the thieves!

"I want to ask my oprichnina: What do you think about this whole issue?"

A grumble is heard in the hall. It's clear what we think! Each wants to have his say. But Batya raises his hand. We quiet down. Batya says:

"Your Majesty, our hearts tremble with anger. It wasn't the Chinese who invented the Tan Xu buy-up. You, Your Majesty, in

* Patronage.

your heartfelt goodness, you have taken care of our friendly Celestial neighbors, but enemies from the western Siberian districts are weaving their wily webs. They are working with a *pink* minister, with an ambassadorial, and along with customs they invented the Tan Xu buy-up."

"True! That's right! Work and Word! We Live to Serve!" sound numerous voices.

Nechai jumps up, a Moscow-born oprichnik who has skinned more than one cat in his time:

"Work and Word! Your Majesty! When the Ambassadorial Department was purged last year, the *extremist* Shtokman confessed on the rack that Tsvetov personally pushed On the Four Taxes in the Duma, and drilled the assessors! It makes one wonder, Your Majesty: Why is that cur so interested in On the Four Taxes now?"

Sterna jumps up:

"Your Majesty, it seems to me that On the Four Taxes is a good law. There's only one thing that's not clear—why 'four'? Where did this number come from? Why not six? Why not eight?"

Our oprichniks buzz:

"Sterna, mind what you say!"

"True, it's true what he says!"

"The number four isn't the problem!"

"No, four is the problem!"

Svirid, older and experienced, stands up:

"Your Majesty, what would change if another number was written in the law? For example, a Chinese family would have not four assessments, but eight? Would the tax assessment increase twofold? No! But why, one wonders? Because they wouldn't let it increase! The clerks. That's what!"

The oprichniks mutter and clamor:

"True! You speak to the point, Svirid! The enemies aren't in China, but in the departments!"

At this point I can't restrain myself:

"Your Majesty! On the Four Taxes is a good law, only it has been diverted in the wrong direction: the district police officers don't need regular business petitions, but *black* mortgages. That's where they're going with this law!"

The right *wing* approves:

"That's right, Komiaga! The law isn't the problem!"

But the left *wing* objects:

"The problem isn't the mortgages, but the law!"

From the left *wing* Buben jumps up: "Chinese can handle six taxes! Russia will only gain from this! Your Majesty, the law needs to be rewritten with another number, to increase the assessments, then they won't travel to pawn things—they won't have time to straighten their backs!"

A lot of noise:

"True!"

"Not true!"

Then Potyka stands up; he's young, but he's tenacious when it comes to guile.

"Your Majesty, I see it this way. Whether there are six assessments or eight, this is what could happen. The Chinese have big families; they'll begin to split and to divide, they'll register by twos and threes, to reduce the tax. And then they'll all mortgage one place, but not as contract workers anymore—instead, as single parasites. Then, by law they can turn in the tax to us by halves. We take two parts, set ourselves up on the third, and the rest will disappear back to the Chinese. It'll turn out that they're all sitting on the tax, bag and baggage. That sort of Chinese guy will marry one of our women—and then there's no Chinese tax assessment at all! He's a citizen of Russia!"

The room is abuzz. Good for Potyka! He sees to the root of things. It wasn't in vain that he served in the Far Eastern customs before the oprichnina. Batya bangs his fist on the table with pleasure.

His Majesty says nothing. He looks at us from the ceiling with his attentive gray-blue gaze. We calm down. Once again silence reigns in the hall. His Majesty speaks:

"Well, I have listened to your opinions. I thank you. I'm glad that my oprichnina is as sharp as ever. I will make a decision about the law on taxes tomorrow. But today I'm taking another decision: to purge the district councils."

A roar of approval. Thank God! Those western Siberian thieves will finally get what they deserve!

We all jump up, pull our daggers out of their sheaths, and lift them:

"Hail! Purge!"

"Hail the Purge!"

"Hail the Purge!"

With a sweeping gesture we stick our daggers in the tables, and clap our hands so hard that the chandeliers shake.

"Hail the Sweep of the Broom!"

"Hail the Sweep to Their Doom!!"

"Hail and Sweep Them Clean!"

Batya's resounding voice thunders:

"Sweep them clean out! Sweep them clean out!"

We take up the cry:

"Sweep them out! Sweep them out!"

We clap till our hands hurt.

His Majesty's face disappears.

Batya lifts his glass:

"To His Majesty's health! Hail!"

"Hail! Hail!"

We drink and sit down.

"Thank God, we'll have work!" grunts Shelet.

"It's long overdue!" I put my knife back in its sheath.

"The councils out there are seething with maggots!" Pravda shakes his gold forelock indignantly.

Rumbling fills the refectory.

A conversation flares up at Batya's table. The fat chairman of the All-Russian Society for the Observance of Human Rights throws up his plump hands:

"My good men! How long must our great Russia bow and cringe before China?! Just as we bowed before foul America during the Time of Troubles, so now we crawl hunchbacked before the Celestial Kingdom. Imagine, His Majesty worries about the Chinese paying their taxes properly!"

Churilo Volodevich seconds him:

"You speak the truth, Anton Bogdanych! They've crammed themselves into our very own Siberia, and we have to worry about their taxes to boot! They should pay us more!"

The bath attendant Mamona shakes his bald head:

"His Majesty's goodness knows no bounds."

The paraxyliarch strokes his gray beard:

"Those border predators feed off His Majesty's kindness. All those insatiable mouths!"

Batya takes a bite of the turkey leg, chews, and holds the leg over the table:

"Where do you think this comes from?"

"From over there, Batya!" Shelet smiles.

"That's right, from over there," Batya continues. "And not only meat. We even eat Chinese bread."

"We drive Chinese Mercedovs," says Pravda, grinning, his teeth showing.

"We fly on Chinese Boeings," Porokhovshchikov interjects.

The game warden nods. "His Majesty likes to shoot ducks with Chinese guns."

"We make children on Chinese beds!" Potyka exclaims.

"We do our business on Chinese toilets!" I add.

Everyone laughs. And Batya lifts his index finger wisely:

"All true! And as long as that's the way things are, we should befriend China and keep the peace, not make war and fight. His Majesty is wise, he sees to the root of things. But you, Anton Bogdanych, even though you're supposed to be a statesman, your reason only touches the surface of things."

"I feel bad for our country!" The chairman turns his round head such that his triple chin jiggles like meat jelly.

"Our state isn't going anywhere, don't worry. The main thing, as His Majesty says, is for each of us to toil honestly in his place for the good of the Motherland. Is that right?"

"True!" we echo Batya.

"Now, since that's true—let's drink to Rus! To Rus!"

"To Rus! Hail! To Rus! To Rus!"

Everyone jumps up. Glasses meet with a ring. Before we've even drunk everything, there's a new toast. Buben shouts:

"To our Batya! Hail!"

"Hail! Hail!"

"To our dearest Batya! Good health to you! Success against opponents. Strength! May your eyes be ever sharp-sighted!"

We drink to our leader. Batya sits there, chews, washes the wine down with kvass. He winks at us. And *suddenly*, he locks his two pinkie fingers together.

The bathhouse!

Oh, Mamochka! My heart flares: Did I imagine it? No! Batya's pinkies are locked together. Those who need to, see the sign. What news! The bathhouse is usually on Saturday, and even then not every Saturday . . . My heart is thumping, I glance at Shelet and Pravda: it's news to them, too! They turn around, chuckle, scratch their beards, twirl their mustaches. Freckled Posokha winks at me and grins wide.

Wonderful! My exhaustion disappears. The baths! I look at the clock—23:12. A whole forty-eight minutes to wait. No matter! We can wait, Komiaga. Time moves on—and man puts up with it. Thank God . . .

The clock in the hall strikes midnight. The end of the oprichniks' evening repast. We all stand. In a loud voice Batya thanks the Lord for our food. We cross ourselves and bow. Our guys head for the exit. But not everyone. The *inner* oprichniks stay—what we call the oprich of the oprichniks. And I'm among them. My heart thumps in anticipation. Sweet, oh how sweet is its beating! In the emptied hall where the servants quickly bustle about, the two *wings* remain, along with the most adroit, outstanding young oprichniks—Okhlop, Potyka, Komol, Yelka, Avila, Obdul, Varyony, and Igla. All first-class—blood with milk, gold-forelock fire fellows.

Batya walks from the large hall to the small hall. We follow him—the right *wing*, the left, and the young people. The servants close the door behind us. Batya approaches the fireplace decorated with three bronze warriors, and pulls Ilya Muromets by his cudgel. A door opens in the wall next to the fireplace. Batya is the first to step through the door, and we follow by rank. As soon as I enter, the bathhouse smell hits my nostrils. And from the very aroma of it my head spins, the blood in my temples beats with little silver hammers: Batya's bath!

We descend the dim stone staircase, down, down, down.

Each step down is a gift, the expectation of *joy*. There is just one thing I can't understand—why Batya decided to have the baths tonight. Will wonders never cease?! Earlier today we enjoyed the golden sterlets—and now we're also going to *take the steam*.

The light flares: the dressing room opens. Batya's bath attendants meet us—Ivan, Zufar, and Cao. They're older, experienced, *trustworthy*. They're all different in personality and blood, and in their bathhouse skills. Only injury unites them: Zufar and Cao are mute, and Ivan is deaf. This is wise not only for Batya, but for them as well—the oprichniks' bathhouse attendants sleep a deeper sleep and live longer.

We sit down and disrobe. The attendants help Batya to undress. And he doesn't lose any time:

"About work. Who has what?"

The left *wingers* are ahead right away: Vosk and Seryi finally got underground Kitaigorod away from the treasurers; now we control all the construction. Nechai has two denunciations against Prince Oboluev, Buben has the money from a deal that was bought off. In Amsterdam, Baldokhai *correctly* rubbed up against the Russian community, and brought back *black* petitions; Samosya's asking for personal damages—he smashed a Streltsy car. Without a single word of reproach, Batya gives him five hundred rubles in gold.

Our fellows from the right *wing* weren't so resourceful today: Mokry fought with tradesmen for the Odintsov Paradise restaurant, but hasn't gotten very far yet; Posokha tortured criminal pilots with the departmentals; Shelet had meetings in the Ambassadorial Department. Yerokha flew to Urengoi to deal with *white* gas; Pravda arranged surveillance and set fire to the apartment of someone in *disgrace*. I'm the only one with a profit:

"Here, Batya, Kozlova bought a half-deal. Twenty-five hundred."

Batya takes the purse, shakes it, unties it, counts out ten gold pieces, and gives me my *due*. He sums up the day:

"In the black."

Other oprichnik days are "festive," "wealthy," "hot," "disbursed," "losing," and "sour." The young people sit and listen, learning a bit of wisdom.

The money and the papers disappear into the white square shining on the wall of the old storeroom. The bath attendants take off Batya's pants. He slaps his hands on his knees:

"I have some news for you, gentlemen oprichniks: Count Andrei Vladimirovich Urusov *is naked*."

We sit there, dumbstruck. Baldokhai is the first to open his mouth:

"How's that, Batya?"

"He's been removed from all his posts by His Majesty's decree, and his accounts frozen. But that's not all."

Our commander takes us all in with his searching gaze:

"His Majesty's daughter, Anna Vasilevna, has sued for divorce from Count Urusov."

Now there you go! That really is news! His Majesty's family! I can't refrain:

"Motherfucker!"

Batya immediately socks me in the jaw.

"Shameless!"

"Forgive me, Batya, the devil made me do it, I couldn't help . . ."

"Fuck your own mother, it will be less expensive."

"Batya, you know my mother passed away . . ." I try *to get him* on pity.

"Fuck her in the grave."

I'm silent as I wipe my split lip with my undershirt.

"I'll beat the brazen, rabble-rousing spirit out of you!" Batya threatens us. "Whoever fouls his lips with curses—will not stay long in the oprichnina!"

We grow quiet.

"So, then," he continues. "His Majesty's daughter has filed for divorce. I don't think the patriarch will divorce them. But the Moscow Metropolitan could divorce them."

He could. We understand. He very likely would. Just like that! If that happened, Urusov would be completely *naked*. How wisely His Majesty conducts internal politics; oh, how wisely! If you look at it from the family point of view, what does that pasquinade mean for him? Underground rebels write all sorts of things . . . After all, no matter what you say, it's his son-in-law, the spouse of his beloved daughter. And if you look at it from the governmental point of view, it's an enviable resolution. Cunning! No wonder His Majesty prefers skittles and chess to all other games. He calculated a multistep combination, drew back, and swung the bat at his own. Knocked a *fattened* son-in-law out of the Inner Circle. And immediately strengthened the people's love for him two- or threefold. Gave the Inner Circle something to think about: don't go too far. He reigned in the departmental clerks: that's how a statesman should act. He energized us, the oprichniks: in the New Russia no one is untouchable. No one is and no one can be. And thank God.

Both *wings* sit shaking their heads, clicking their tongues:

"Urusov—*naked*. Hard to believe!"

"There you go! Turned Moscow topsy-turvy!"

"He shone in His Majesty's favor."

"He stirred things up, shuffled people around."

"Drove three Rolls-Royces."

It's true—Urusov had three Rolls-Royces: gold, silver, and platinum.

"So what's he gonna drive now?" Yerokha asks.

"A lame electric goat!" Zamosya answers.

We chuckle.

"Well, that's not the last bit of news," says Batya, standing up naked.

"He's coming here. To the baths. To take the steam and ask for our protection."

Those standing sit down again. This is too much! Urusov—coming to see Batya? On the other hand, if you think about it rationally, where else does he have to hide, now that he's *naked*? His Majesty kicked him out of the Kremlin, businessmen will flee from him, the departmentals as well. As a fornicator, the Patriarch won't shelter him. To Buturlin? They can't stand each other. To Her Highness? Her stepdaughter despises her for "debauchery," she hates her stepdaughter and her stepdaughter's husband, even though he's already a *former* one, all the more. The road to China is closed for the count: Zhou Shen Min is a friend of His Majesty and won't go against his will. What can the count do? Sit in his estate and wait for us to roll up with our brooms? So, out of desperation, he decides to pay obeisance to Batya. That's the right thing to do! For a *naked* man the road can lead only to the bathhouse.

"So that's the way the cookie crumbles and the chips fly," Batya sums up. "And now—to the baths!"

Batya is the first to enter. Naked, like Adam, we follow him. Batya's bathhouse is rich: the ceilings are vaulted and abutted by columns; the floor is marble mosaic; the pool is large; the lounge chairs comfortable. The aroma of bread is already coming from the steam room—Batya likes to use kvass for his steam.

He immediately commands:

"Right *wing*!"

Batya is commander in chief in his bathhouse. We rush to the steam room. Ivan is already waiting there in his felt cap and gloves, with two bunches of twigs—birch and oak. The carousel begins: we lie down on the sweating shelves, deaf Ivan starts the kvass steam, grunts, and chants an unusually loud jokey jingle as he begins to lash the oprichniks with the birch brooms.

I lie there, my eyes closed. I wait my turn, breathing in the steam. Then the waiting is over: whisk, whisk, whisk—on my back, my ass, my legs. Ivan is so experienced in bath whipping it's unbelievable—he doesn't stop until you're steam-cleaned. But at Batya's you shouldn't steam too long, for *other* pleasures lie in store. Even in the steam room my heart grows cold in anticipation.

Ivan steams away, chanting:

"Hark, hark,
Grind beans and bark
Yurop to gas
With oprichnik ass.

"Ass bone white,
Works day and night,
Smear it with lard,
Show Yurop what's hard!"

Ivan's little ditty is old, and he's not too young himself: there's *no one* in Europe to show a Russian ass to anyway. No decent people remain beyond the Western Wall, only Arab cyberpunks crawling over the ruins. Europe or an ass, it's all the same to them.

Oak branches rustle on the nape of my neck, and birch branches tickle my heels.

"Ready!"

I climb off the shelf and fall into Zufar's strong hands: now it's his turn. He grabs me like a sack of potatoes, hoists me over his back, and lugs me out of the steam room. Taking a running start, he chucks me into the pool. Oh, I feel good! Everything is top-notch at Batya's—the steam is hot and the water ice-cold. It goes straight to the bone. I swim, and wake up. But Zufar doesn't give you a breather—he pulls me up, tosses me onto the futon, jumps on my back, and starts walking on me. My vertebrae crack. His Tatar feet walk along a Russian spine. They walk skillfully—they do no harm, won't destroy, won't bruise . . . His Majesty knows how to join all the peoples of the Russian land under his mighty wing: the Tatars and Mordovians, Bashkir, Jews, Chechens, Ingush, Cheremis, the Evenki and Yakuts, the Marii, Karelians, Buriats, Urdmurts, the simple-hearted Chukchi, and many, many others.

Zufar pours water over me and gives me to Cao. And now I'm reclining in the washroom, looking at the painted ceiling, and the Chinese Cao is washing me. His soft, quick fingers slip over my body, rub fragrant foam into my hair, pour aromatic oils on my stomach; he runs his fingers through my toes, and massages my calves. No one can wash you like a Chinese. They know how to handle the human body. On the ceiling there's a scene of a heavenly garden; birds and beasts, heeding the voice of God. Man isn't in this garden yet—he hasn't been created. It's lovely to look at the garden of paradise when you're being washed. Something long-ago forgotten awakens in your soul, something drawn out by the lard of time . . .

Cao splashes cool water on me from the lime flower washtub, and helps me to stand. You feel heartened and *ready* after a Chinese bath. I walk into the main hall. Gradually, everyone joins, passing through the Russian-Tatar-Chinese conveyor. Clean, rosy bodies plop down on the lounge beds, swigging nonalcoholic drinks, chatting. Uzh, Shelet, and Samosya have already been through the steam room; Mokry just got wet; Vosk collapsed on the lounge with a grunt; and Yerokha is oohing and aahing in gratitude. Chapyzh and Buben down the kvass greedily, coming to their senses. Great is the brotherhood of the bathhouse. Everyone is equal here—the right and the left, the old and the young. Gilded forelocks have gotten wet and tousled. Tongues have loosened:

"Samosya, so where d'ya hit that colonel anyway?"

"I smashed his side at the turn from Ostozhenka. That Streltsy idiot chickened out, wouldn't get out of the car. Then their people came with a *square*, a *hand*, the duty policeman *folded*, I didn't pass for a good guy, and I didn't want to butt heads with a cudgel . . ."

"Brothers, listen, a new joint opened on Maroseika Street—called Kissel Shores. Pretty expensive: twelve kinds of *kissel*, vodka made from lime-tree buds, hare in noodles, girls singing . . ."

"For Shrovetide His Majesty is giving presents to athletes: a hydrogen Mercedov apiece; *gorodki* players get a fat-tailed motorcycle, the women archers a viviparous fur coat . . ."

"In short, the SOBs locked themselves in, and Batya forbade us to use fireworks—the house wasn't in disgrace. Couldn't use gas or lasers either. So we did things the old way—in the lower quarter: this and that, the enemies are upstairs. We asked them statesman-like, officially, they came out with suitcases and icons, we singed them, began to smoke the upstairs ones out. We thought they'd open up, but they jumped out the window. The elder landed on the fence—the spike went straight through his liver—the younger broke his leg but survived, and then he gave evidence . . ."

"Avdotia Petrovna personally broke the toilets with her humongous ass, I swear . . ."

"Yerokha, hey, Yerokha . . ."

"Whaddya want?"

"Where's my pie?"

"You knucklehead! Pick up your balls, they're rolling around on the floor!"

"Buben, is it true that *gray* profits in the Trade Department are being closed down through the tax collectors?"

"Unh-uh. Only bonuses go through the tax collectors, but the *gray* are still *covered* by the junior clerks."

"There's enemies for you! No poker made could ever pick them out . . ."

"Wait until the fall, Brother Okhlop. We'll pick them all out."

"Autumn, autumn, they're burning shiiiips . . . young man, where did you get your tattoo?"

"In Nebuchadnezzar."

"That's nice. Especially down below, with the dragons . . ."

"Come on, Brother Mokry, let me have a swig of kvass."

"Swig as much as you want, for the love of Christ, Brother Potyka."

"They keep on about bribes, bribes, bribes . . . what the hell do I need to dig up bribes for?"

"See-saw, saw-see, Brother Yerokha doesn't like me . . ."

"I'll crack your forehead open, you troublemaker!"

"Did you hear why His Majesty closed the Third Western Pipeline? Those shithead Europeans didn't give the court any Château Lafite again; just half a car, and they can't even get that together!"

As always, Batya is the last into the steam room. The bath-house attendants hold his wide body up and bring him to us. They hand over our kinsman:

"Batya, we hope you enjoyed your bath!"

"We hope it went all the way to the bone!"

"To your health!"

"Into the backbone."

"Into the marrow!"

Batya's body gives off heat.

"Oof, Holy Mother of God . . . give me some kvass!"

Silver cups are held out to our beloved Batya.

"Drink, Brother Batya!"

Batya scans us with bleary eyes, making his choice:

"Vosk!"

Vosk holds the cup for Batya. Of course, today the left *wing* is in favor. Rightly so. They earned it.

Batya drains the cup of honey kvass, takes a breath, and belches. He looks us over. *We freeze.* Batya bides his time, winks at us. And utters the *long-awaited* "Cluck, cluck cluck!"

The light goes down, and from the marble wall a shining hand, full of pills, extends outward. And like the confession for the Holy Communion, we stand in a humble line at the illumined palm. Each of us approaches, takes his tablet, places it in his mouth under the tongue, and moves away. I do the same. I take the tablet, which doesn't look like anything unusual. I place it in my mouth, and already my fingers are trembling, my knees are weak, and my heart is beating like an anxious hammer; my blood is pounding at my temples like oprichniks breaking into a Zemstvo estate.

My trembling tongue covers the tablet as a cloud covers a temple high atop a hill. The tablet melts, melts sweetly under the tongue, the saliva flooding down upon it like the River Jordan flows in springtime. My heart throbs, I gasp for breath, the ends of my fingers grow cold, and my eyes are more sharp-sighted in the gloom. And now comes the long-awaited moment: a rush of blood to my member. I lower my eyes. I behold it, filling with blood. My refurbished member—with two cartilaginous inserts, a blade of hyperfilaments, pellets in bas relief—rises like a wave of meat with moving tattoos. It levitates like the trunk of a Siberian mammoth. And under my bold member the crimson light of my weighty genitals begins to glow. And not only mine. The genitals of everyone who took communion from the shining palm are glowing, like fireflies in rotten tree stumps on Midsummer's Eve. The oprichniks' genitals have been kindled, each with its own light. For the right *wing* this color ranges from scarlet to the dark murrey of blood; for the left from sky blue to violet; and for the greenhorns, green light of all hues. And it is only our Batya whose genitals shine a special color, distinct from all the others—our dear Batya's genitals shine yellow-gold. The great strength of the oprichnik brotherhood lies here. Oprichniks all have genitals revamped by ingenious Chinese doctors. Light flows from the genitals, craving manly love. It gathers strength from the rising member. And until the light has waned— we, the oprichniks, are entwined in brotherly embraces. Strong hands grasp strong bodies. We kiss one another on the lips. We kiss silently, like men, without any women's sweet talk. We greet and excite one another through our kissing. The bath attendants bustle among us with clay pots filled with Chinese ointments. We scoop out the thick, aromatic ointment and spread it on our members. The wordless attendants move to and fro among us like shadows, for they do not shine.

"Hail!" Batya exclaims.

"Hail, hail!" we cry.

Batya is the *first* to rise. He moves Vosk close to him. Vosk sticks his member in Batya's asshole. Batya groans with pleasure, grins, and bares his white teeth. Shelet embraces Vosk, pokes his greased dick in him. Vosk lets out a belly screech. Seryi fills up Shelet; Seryi is speared by Samosya, Samosya by Baldokhai, Baldokhai by Mokry, Mokry by Nechai, who has to push his sticky stud in, and then my turn comes. I clasp the left-*wing* brother with my left hand, and with my right I direct my member into his asshole. Wide is Nechai's hole; I drive my member all the way to his purple core. Nechai doesn't even grunt; he's used to it, he's one of the elder oprichniks. I get a stronger grasp on him, press him to me, tickle him with my beard. Buben attaches himself to me. My trembling asshole feels his club. It's large—without a push it won't go in. Buben pushes and pokes, then drives his fat-head member in. His machine reaches all the way to my innards, squeezing a guttural moan out of me. I moan in Nechai's ear. Buben groans in mine, embracing me with his valiant arms. I don't see who sticks him, but by the groans I know—it's a worthy member. Well, there aren't really any unworthy among us—the Chinese have renewed our genitals, strengthened them, equipped them. We have the wherewithal to delight one another, as well as to punish Russia's enemies. The oprichnik *caterpillar* gathers, coupling. Behind me I hear groans and screeches. The law of the brotherhood requires that the left *wingers* and right *wingers* alternate, and only then do the younger ones join together. That's Batya's rule. And thank God . . .

By the cries and muttering I sense that the youngsters' turn has come. Batya cheers them on:

"Don't be scared, greenhorns!"

The youngsters are trying, they long to burst into each other's tight assholes. The *dark* bath attendants help them, they direct them, support them. The next-to-last cries out, the last groans—and the *caterpillar* is ready. It's *complete. We stay stock-still.*

"Hail!" cries Batya.

"Hail! Hail!" we roar in reply.

Batya takes a step. And we follow him, we follow the head of the caterpillar. Batya leads us into the pool. It's spacious, roomy. It's filled with warm water instead of ice water.

"Hail! Hail!" we shout, embracing each other, shuffling.

We follow Batya. We walk. We walk. We walk in *caterpillar* steps. Our genitals glow, our members shudder between buttocks.

We enter the pool. Around us the water boils with air bubbles. Batya submerges himself up to his genitals, then to his waist, his chest. The entire oprichnik *caterpillar* enters the pool. And rises.

Now it's time to be silent. Muscular arms tense, valiant nostrils flare, the oprichniks have begun to moan. The time for the *sweet* work has come. We coax each other. The water ripples around us, waves heave, splashing out of the pool. And now the *long-awaited* moment has come: a tremor rolls through the entire *caterpillar*.

And:

"Haaaaaaaiiiillll!"

The arched ceiling shakes. And the pool—becomes a nine-point storm.

"Haaaaiiiillll!"

I roar into Nechai's ear, and Buben screams into mine:

"Haaaaiiiillll!"

Lord, don't let us die . . .

Indescribable. Because it's so divine.

Reclining on the soft chaise lounges after oprichnik copulation is like the bliss of paradise. The light is on, buckets of champagne sit on the floor, forest air, Rachmaninov's Second Concerto for piano and orchestra. Our Batya likes to listen to the Russian classics after copulation. We lie there weakly. The lights in our genitals go out. We drink silently, catch our breath.

Wisely, oh so wisely, Batya arranged everything with the *caterpillar*. Before it, everyone broke off in pairs, and the shadow of dangerous disorder lay across the oprichnina. Now there's a limit to the pleasures of the steam. We work together, and take our pleasure together. And the tablets help. And wisest of all is that the young oprichniks are always stuck at the tail of the *caterpillar*. This is wise for two reasons: first of all, the young ones know their place in the oprichnik hierarchy; second, the seed moves from the tail of the *caterpillar* to the head, which symbolizes the eternal cycle of life and the renewal of our brotherhood. On the one hand, the young respect the old; on the other, they replenish them. That's our foundation. And thank God.

It's pleasant to sip Szechuan champagne, feeling how healthy oprichnik seed soaks into the walls of the large intestine. Health isn't the least thing in our dangerous life. I take care of mine: I play skittles twice a week, then I swim, I drink maple juice with ground wild strawberries, I eat overgrown fern seeds, I breathe properly. Other oprichniks strengthen their bodies as well.

Batya is informed from above that Count Urusov has appeared. The bath attendants hand out sheets to everyone. Covering our *extinguished* private parts, we lie back on our chairs. The count enters from the bathhouse dressing room. He's wrapped his sheet to look like a Roman toga. The count is a stocky man; he has white skin and thin legs, a large head and short neck. His face, as usual, is gloomy. But something *new* is imprinted on this well-known face.

We look at him silently, as though he were a ghost: previously we saw this man only when we were wearing tuxedos or gold-embroidered caftans.

"Health to you, oprichniks," the count says in a flat voice.

"Health to you, Count," we answer separately.

Batya, lying on his chaise, says nothing. The count's mirthless eyes find him:

"Hello, Boris Borisovich."

And . . . he bows to the waist.

Our jaws drop. Now that's heavy. Count Urusov the mighty, all-powerful, unapproachable, bowing to the waist in front of our Batya. Makes you remember the ancient: *sic transit gloria mundi.*

Batya takes his time standing up.

"To your health, Count."

He bows in reply, crosses his arms on his stomach, and looks at the count silently. Our Batya is a head taller than Urusov.

"So then, I decided to visit you," the count says, breaking the silence. "I'm not intruding, am I?"

"We're always happy to have guests," says Batya. "There's still some steam."

"I'm not terribly keen on steam baths. I have a pressing matter to discuss with you, one that will brook no delay. Shall we retire to a more private setting?"

"I have no secrets from the oprichniks, Count," Batya answers calmly, making a sign to the attendants. "Champagne?"

The glum count purses his lips, glances at us sideways with the eyes of a wolf. And he is a wolf—only exhausted, at bay. Cao brings them champagne. Batya takes a slender glass, gulps it down, puts it back on the tray, and grunts as he wipes his mustache. Urusov only puts his lips to the glass, as though it were hemlock.

"We're listening, dear Andrei Vladimirovich!" Batya says in a loud voice. He lowers himself onto his chaise lounge again. "Lie down, don't be shy."

The count sits sideways on the chaise and locks his fingers together:

"Boris Borisovich, you're aware of my situation?"

"I'm aware."

"I fell from grace."

Batya nods. "It happens."

"To what extent, I don't yet know. But I hope that sooner or later His Majesty will forgive me."

Batya nods again. "His Majesty is merciful."

"I have a proposition for you. My accounts are frozen by His Majesty's decree, and my trade and manufacturing properties have been expropriated, but His Majesty left me my personal property."

"Thank God." Batya belches Chinese carbon dioxide.

The count looks at his well-groomed nails, touches his ring with the diamond hedgehog, and pauses. Then he speaks:

"I have an estate near Moscow, in the Pereyaslavsky district, and one near Voronezh, in Divnogor. And of course the house on Piatnitsky Street, you've been there . . ."

"I've been there." Batya inhales.

"So this is the offer, Boris Borisovich. I give the house on Piatnitsky to the oprichnina."

Silence. Batya says nothing. Urusov says nothing. Nor do we. Cao freezes with an uncorked bottle of Szechuan champagne in his hand. Urusov's house on Piatnitsky . . . It's shameful to even call it a house: it's a palace! Columns of layered marble, a roof with sculpture and vases, openwork grills, gatekeepers with halberds, stone lions . . . I haven't been inside, but it isn't hard to imagine that it's even more incredible inside. They say that the count's drawing room floor is transparent, and that under it—there's an aquarium with sharks. And all the sharks are striped like tigers. How inventive!

"The house on Piatnitsky." Batya squints. "Why such a valuable gift?"

"It isn't a gift. You and I are businesspeople. I give you the house, you give me a roof over my head, *protection*. When I'm back in good graces—I'll add more. I won't forget you."

"It's a serious proposition," says Batya, squinting and casting his gaze over us. "We'll have to discuss it. All right, who's first?"

The sophisticated Vosk raises his hand.

"Why don't we hear the young ones first." Batya glances at the youngest. "All right?"

The ever alert Potyka raises his hand.

"If you'll permit me, Batya!"

"Go on, Potyka, speak."

"Forgive me, Batya, but it seems to me that there's no benefit for us in protecting dead men. Because a dead man doesn't care whether there's a roof over his head or not. For that matter, it's not a roof he needs, but a coffin."

Silence hangs in the bathhouse. It's silent as the grave. The count turns green. Batya smacks his lips:

"So you see, Count. Note that this is the voice of our young people. You can imagine what the elder oprichniks would have to say about your proposition?"

The count licks his bloodless lips:

"Listen, Boris. You and I aren't children. What dead man? What coffin? So I fell under His Majesty's hot hand, but it's not forever! His Majesty knows how much I've done for Russia! A year will pass—and he'll forgive me! And you'll still have the profit!"

Batya frowns:

"You think he'll forgive you?"

"I'm certain."

"Oprichniks, what do you think: Will His Majesty forgive the count or not?"

"No-o-o-o," we answer in unison.

Batya's hands gesture in dismay.

"You see?"

"Listen!" the count jumps up. "Stop fooling around! I don't have time for jokes! I've lost almost everything! But I swear to God—everything will be returned! Everything will be returned!"

Batya sighs and stands up, leaning on Ivan:

"You're just like Job, Count. Everything will be returned . . . But nothing will be returned to you. And you know why? Because you placed your lust higher than the state."

"Boris, don't go too far!"

"I'm not taking anything too far." Batya walks up to the count. "You think His Majesty is angry because you like to fornicate in fire? Because you're shaming his daughter? No. That's not why. You burned state property. Therefore, you took a step against the state. Against His Majesty."

"Bobrinskaya's house is her own property! What does His Majesty have to do with it?!"

"You blockhead, what he has to do with it is that we are all

His Majesty's children, and all of our property belongs to him! The whole country is his! You of all people should know that! Life hasn't taught you anything, Andrei Vladimirovich. You were His Majesty's son-in-law, but you became a rebel. And not just a rebel, but a son of a bitch. Rotten, dead meat."

The count's eyes flash with dark fury:

"What?! You cur, you . . ."

Batya puts two fingers in his mouth and whistles. And as though by command, the young guys rush the count and grab him.

"Into the pool with him!" Batya orders.

The oprichniks tear the sheet off the count and throw him into the pool. The count comes up, sputtering:

"You'll answer for this, you dogs, you'll answer . . ."

All of a sudden knives appear in the youngsters' hands. Now that's new! It should be clear to you now, you dolt! Why didn't I know? Curtains for the count? They gave the go-ahead?

The youngsters stand around the edge of the pool.

"Haaiiillll!" cries Batya.

"Hail, hail!" cry the youngsters.

"Hail, hail!" the rest of us take up the cry.

"Death to the enemies of Russia!" Batya exclaims.

"Death! Death! Death!" we continue the chant.

The count swims up to the edge of the pool, and grabs on to the marble. But on the other side, Komol strikes with a flourish: his knife flies like lightning, piercing the count's stooped back up to its handle. The count lets out a furious wail. Okhlop waves his hand—and his knife flies, landing right next to the first. Yelka and Avila aim their knives—just as precisely, also at the back of the *naked* count. He screams with fury and indignation. How much anger that bastard has stored up. The knives of the remaining youngsters fly into him. And all of them hit their target. They know how to aim knives, those lads. We old-timers prefer to use our knives closer up.

The count no longer wails; he's wheezing, tossing and turning in the water. He looks like a sea mine.

"There's 'everything will be returned' for you." Batya grins, taking a glass from the tray and sipping it.

A convulsion passes through the count's body, and he stiffens forever. Life and fate.

"Upstairs with him." Batya nods to the bath attendants. "Change the water."

The attendants drag Urusov's corpse out of the pool, take the gold cross and the famous hedgehog ring off him, and give them to Batya. Batya tosses what remains of the powerful count in his hand.

"There you have it: here and gone!"

They take out the corpse. Batya gives the gold cross to Svirid:

"Give this to our church tomorrow."

He puts the hedgehog ring on his pinkie.

"We've had our steam bath. Upstairs! Everyone—upstairs!"

The grandfather clock strikes 02:30. We're sitting in the tiled drawing room. After midnight Batya has kept only five of us: Potyka, Vosk, Baldokhai, Yerokha, and me. After the *wet stuff* our Batya had a hankering for *coke* with vodka. We sit at a round table of red granite. There's a dish with stripes of white, candles, and a carafe of vodka. Yerokha warms the dish with the candle, drying the *coke* from below. Batya's already loaded, and when he's really loaded, he likes to give us lofty lectures. Our dear Batya has three speeches: one about His Majesty, one about his deceased mama, and one about the Christian faith. Today it's faith:

"Now you, my dear Enochs, you're wondering, why was the Wall built, why are we fenced off, why did we burn our foreign passports, why are there different classes, why were intelligent machines changed to Cyrillic? To increase profits? To maintain order? For entertainment? For home and hearth? To create the big and beautiful? For fancy houses? For Moroccan leather boots, so everyone could tap their heels and clap? For all that's good, true, and well made, so that there'd be plenty all around? To make the state as mighty as a pole from the heavenly tamarind tree? So that it supports the heavenly vault and the stars, goddamnit, so the stars and moon would shine, you sniveling scarecrow wolves, so that the warm wind would blow-not-stop-blowing on your asses, is that it? So your asses would stay nice and warm in your velvet pants? So your heads would feel cozy under their sable hats? So you sniveling wolves wouldn't live by lies? So you'd run in herds, fast, straight, close together, most holy, obedient, so you'd harvest the grain on time, feed your brother, love your wives and children, is that it?"

Batya pauses, inhales a good snort of white *coke* and washes it down with vodka. We do the same thing.

"Now you see, my dearest Enochs, that's not what it was for. It was so the Christian faith would be preserved like a chaste treasure, you get it? For only we, the Orthodox, have preserved the church as Christ's body on earth, a single church, sacred, conciliar, apostolic, and infallible, isn't that right? After the Second Nicene Council we are the only ones who glorify the Lord correctly, for we are Russian Orthodox, because no one took the right to glorify the Lord correctly away from us, did they? We didn't retreat from the community of our church, from sacred icons, from the Mother of God, from the faith of the fathers, from the life-giving Trinity, from the Holy Spirit, from the life-giving Lord who comes from the Father, who venerates the Father and Son and speaks the prophet, right? We have rejected everything sacrilegious: Manichaeanism, and Monotheletism, and Monophysitism, right? For whomsoever the church is not mother, God is not the father, right? For God by His nature is beyond understanding, right? For all true-believing Orthodox priests are heirs of Peter, right? For there is no purgatory, only hell and heaven, right? For man is born mortal and therefore he sins, right? For God is the light, right? For our Savior became human so that you and I, sniveling wolves, could become gods, right? That's why His Majesty built this magnificent Wall, in order to cut us off from stench and unbelievers, from the damned cyberpunks, from sodomites, Catholics, melancholiacs, from Buddhists, sadists, Satanists, and Marxists; from megamasturbators, fascists, pluralists, and atheists! For faith, you sniveling wolves, isn't a change purse! It's no brocaded caftan! No oak club! What is faith? Faith, my noisy ones—is a well of springwater, pure, clear, quiet, modest, powerful, and plentiful! You get it? Or should I repeat it to you?"

"We got it, Batya," we always answer.

"Well, then, if you got it—thank the Lord."

Batya crosses himself. We cross ourselves as well. We snort some more. Wash it down. Groan.

And suddenly Yerokha's nostrils sniffle with hurt.

"What is it?" Batya turns to him.

"Forgive me, Batya, if I say something that might cross you."

"Well?"

"I'm offended."

"What offends you, Brother Yerokha?"

"That you put the noble's ring on your finger."

Yerokha is talking sense. Batya squints at him. Then he says loudly:

"Trofim!"

Batya's servant appears:

"What do you desire, sir?"

"An axe!"

"Yes, sir."

We sit, looking at one another. And Batya takes a look at us and suppresses a smile. Trofim comes back with the axe. Batya takes the ring off his finger, and places it on the granite table:

"Go ahead!"

Faithful Trofim understands immediately: he picks up the axe and smashes the ring. Splinters of diamond fly.

"There you go!" Batya laughs.

We laugh as well. That's our Batya. That's what we love him for, why we cherish him, and remain faithful to him. He blows the diamond dust off the table:

"So what are your mouths hanging open for? Go on and cut it!"

Potyka takes care of the *coke*, cuts the lines. I wanted to ask why the youngsters were involved with the count but we elders were in the dark. We weren't needed? Lost our trustworthiness? But I hold back: better not to ask in the heat of the moment. I'll get to Batya *from below* by and by . . .

And suddenly Baldokhai says:

"Batya, who wrote that pasquinade?"

"Filka the Rhymester."

"Who's that?"

"A talented guy. He's going to be working for us . . ." Batya leans over and sucks a white strip through his bone tube. "He wrote a great one about His Majesty. Want to hear it? Hey, Trofim, call him."

Trofim dials the number, and a sleepy, scared face in glasses appears not far away.

"Taking a nap?" Batya says, drinking from a shot glass.

"No, no, Boris Borisovich . . ." the rhymester mutters.

"Come on, then, read us the poem to His Majesty."

The fellow straightens his glasses, clears his throat, and recites with feeling:

In our time, far distant and remote,
Behind the stone wall of the ancients,
Lives not a man, but Creation:
An act, a deed, as great as earth's own globe.

Fate has given him his lot,
Which does precede the very void.
He is what all the boldest dream of,
Though none before has dared or thought.

But he remains a human being,
And should he come across a winter wolf,
He'll shoot, and his shot, too, will echo in the woods,
As surely as it does for you and me.

Batya pounds his fist on the table:

"Well? Son of a bitch! See how cleverly he wrapped it up, huh?"

We agree:

"Clever."

"All right, go back to sleep, Filka!" Batya says, turning him off.

Suddenly Batya begins singing in a deep bass:

The hour of grief, the hour of parting
I want to share, with you my friend.
Let's drill right through our legs while farting,
And walk ahead, until the road does end.

I'd been hoping we'd avoid this today, that Batya would collapse before things came to it. But our commander is steadfast: after *coke* and vodka he wants to drill. What can you do—if it's drilling, then it's drilling. Not the first time. And there's Trofim: he opens a red box; red bits are laid in it like revolvers. In every brace there's a fine drill of viviparous diamond. I think Batya remembered this *sharp* pastime when the diamond ring was crushed. Trofim hands everyone a drill.

"At my command!" Batya mutters, smashed and stiff. "One, two, three!"

We lower the drills under the table, turn them on, and try to hit someone's leg on the first try. You can stick only one time. If you blow it—don't judge too harshly. I hit the mark—Vosk, it seems—and someone's hit my left leg, probably Batya himself. The drilling begins:

"Hail, hail!"

"Hail, hail!"

"Burn, burn, burn!"

Endure, endure, endure. The drills go through meat like butter, and run into the bone. Endure, endure, endure! We endure, clench our teeth, look at one another:

"Burn! Burn! Burn!"

We withstand, withstand, withstand. The mosquito drills reach the bone marrow. And the first to cave is Potyka:

"Ooooowwww!"

"Break off," Batya commands.

We break off the bits. The tips stay in our legs. Potyka lost: grimacing and whimpering, he grabs his knee. Patience—that's what the youngsters need to learn from us, their elders.

"Vakhrushev!" Batya shouts.

The oprichnik doctor appears, silent Pyotr Sergeevich, with two assistants. They remove the pieces of diamond drill from our legs. The drills are finer than fine, just a bit thicker than a strand of woman's hair. They bandage us up, inject us with medicine. Batya collapses in the arms of servants, hits them on their smackers, sings songs, giggles, farts. As the loser, Potyka hands over all the money he has on him to the oprichnik pot—a couple of hundred in paper and around a hundred and fifty in gold.

"All's well that ends well," Batya roars. "Drivers!"

The servants grab me under the arms and carry me out.

A government driver takes me home in my Mercedov. I'm sprawled out and half asleep. Nighttime Moscow whizzes by. Lights. Moscow's late-night suburbs race by. Firs and roofs. Roofs and firs. Roofirs, dusted with snow. After a full day of work it's good to leave the stern capital behind and return to my dear Moscow woods. To say farewell to Moscow. Because Moscow is the head of all Russia. And the head has a brain. By night the brain tires. And sings in its sleep. And in the singing there's motion: contraction, expansion. Tension. Suspension. Millions and millions of volts and amps create the necessary rate. Energy doctors dwell there. Nuclear bricks flicker. They whistle and align. Together they bind. Stick fast forever and evermore. And man is made from this store. Molecule houses of three rows. Even four or five. Which is wide? Sometimes of eighty-eight. We'll ask them later. And all the houses are behind sturdy fences, they all have guards, the subversive vermin, willful worms, born with silver spoons, for execution doomed. The state cauldrons boil. The fat, fat, fat of those who've met their Maker drips on the snow. Human fat, rendered from a cast iron cauldron brimming over, over, overflow, overflowing. An unending stream of fat pouring flowing out on the snow. It swirls in the bitter cold it swirls. Swirls into frozen mother of pearl. It freezes and sets, sets, sets, sets into a sculpture so beautiful. Sublime. Superb. Inimitable. Splendid. Delightful. The beauty of the fat sculpture is divine and indescribable. The pink, mother-of-pearl fat, tender, cool. Her Highness's breast is cast from the fat of her subjects. The enormous breast of Her Highness! It hangs above us in the blue. It is vast! If only to reach her, fly upward on a swift-winged Chinese airplane, on our enemies' fierce fighter jets, to touch her with my lips, to press against her breast, to press my cheek, press, press, freeze forever, so no cripples or clowns can tear me away, so that no one can pull me off, off the breast, pull me away from Her Highness's breast, nor rip away with red-hot tongs, nor slice off with a knife, nor crack apart with a crowbar, nor break with bones, bones crack loud, the meat bursts, my meat, my flesh, fleeting, corruptible meat, my poor meat, glory to you in the heavens above, glory to you for now and evermore, *mamo*, Our White Fat!

Master, lord and father, Andrei Danilovich!"

I open my eyes. The night-light illuminates Anastasia's tear-stained face. She's holding an ampoule of smelling salts and sticking it up my nose. I push it away, frown, and sneeze:

"Ah, go to . . ."

She looks at me:

"What are you doing to yourself? Why don't you take care of yourself?"

I toss and turn, but don't have the strength to sit up. I remember: she did something bad to me. I can't remember . . . what . . . I'm thirsty:

"Drink!"

She brings a pitcher of white kvass. I drain it. Totally exhausted, I lie back on the pillow. Now the most important thing is to belch. I belch. I feel better immediately:

"What time is it?"

"Four thirty."

"In the morning?"

"In the morning, Andrei Danilovich."

"So, I haven't gone to bed yet?"

"They brought you here unconscious."

"Where's Fedka?"

"I'm here, Andrei Danilovich."

Fedka's gloomy face appears near the bed.

"Did anyone call?"

"No one called."

"What's going on in the house?"

"Nanny got food poisoning from farmer's cheese—she vomited bile. Tanka is asking for Wednesday off to go home for a baptism. The shower is leaking again; I already put a call out on the network. And you need to approve the dog's head for tomorrow, Andrei Danilovich. On account of the one we got now the crows picked to pieces. I have two: a Caucasian sheepdog, fresh, and a Bordeaux Great Dane, frozen, from White Cold. Shall I bring them?"

"Tomorrow. Get out of here."

Fedka disappears. Anastasia turns out the night-light, undresses in the dark, crosses herself, mutters a prayer for the coming night, and lies down with me under the blanket. She nestles her warm body against me, and takes the gold bell out of my earlobe, placing it on the nightstand:

"Will you allow me to love you gently?"

"Tomorrow," I mumble, closing my leaden eyelids.

"As you command, master . . ." she sighs into my ear, caressing my forehead.

She did do something to me, I'm sure of it . . . something not very nice. Something in secret . . . But what? Someone told me today. Where was I today? At Batya's. At the Good Fellows. At Her Highness's. Who else? I forgot.

"Listen, you didn't steal anything from me, did you?"

"Lord almighty . . . What are you saying, Andrei Danilovich?! Lordy!" She sniffles.

"Nastya, where was I today?"

"How should I know, sir? You probably planted your seed in some city missus, and that's why you don't want me anymore. There ain't no need to take it out on an honest girl . . ."

She sobs.

Barely able to turn my leaden arm, I embrace her:

"Now, now, silly girl, I was doing government work, risking my life."

"May you live a hundred years . . ." she mumbles, sobbing in the darkness, her feelings hurt.

Maybe not a hundred, but I'll live awhile longer. We'll live, we'll live. And we'll let others live as well. A passionate, heroic, government life. Important. We have to serve the great ideal. We must live to spite the bastards, to rejoice in Russia . . . My white stallion, wait . . . don't run away . . . where are you going my beloved . . . where, my white-maned . . . my sugar stallion . . . we're alive . . . oh yes, we're alive . . . stallions are alive, people alive . . . all alive till now . . . everyone . . . the entire oprich-nina . . . our entire kindred oprichnina. And as long as the oprichniks are alive, Russia will be alive.

And thank God.

A NOTE ABOUT THE AUTHOR

Vladimir Sorokin was born in 1955. He is the author of many novels, plays, short stories, screenplays, and a libretto. He has won the Andrei Bely Prize and the Maxim Gorky Prize, and was a finalist for the Russian Booker Prize. His work has been translated into many languages. He lives in Moscow.

A NOTE ABOUT THE TRANSLATOR

Jamey Gambrell is a writer on Russian art and culture. Her translations include works by Joseph Brodsky, Alexander Rodchenko, Tatyana Tolstaya, and Marina Tsvetaeva. She has also translated Vladimir Sorokin's *The Ice Trilogy*, his novella *A Month in Dachau*, and a number of his stories. She lives in New York City.